"Who's he?" Darrow bit out the words.

"He's my son," she managed at last. His grip on her arm tightened at her words, but he remained silent, his body rigid with tension.

"I didn't know you had a child." His voice was a harsh whisper, as if some sharp pain was trapped in his throat. "And the father?"

CATHERINE O'CONNOR was born and has lived all her life in Manchester, England, where she is a happily married woman with five demanding children, a neurotic cat, an untrainable dog and a rabbit. She spends most of her time either writing or planning her next story, and without the support and encouragement of her long-suffering husband, this would be impossible. Though her heroes are always wonderfully handsome and incredibly rich, she still prefers her own loving husband.

Sweet
Lies

CATHERINE O'CONNOR

DARK SECRETS

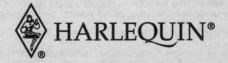

TORONTO • NEW YORK • LONDON
AMSTERDAM • PARIS • SYDNEY • HAMBURG
STOCKHOLM • ATHENS • TOKYO • MILAN • MADRID
PRAGUE • WARSAW • BUDAPEST • AUCKLAND

ISBN 0-373-80542-X

SWEET LIES

First North American Publication 2002.

Copyright © 1996 by Catherine O'Connor.

Visit us at www.eHarlequin.com

Printed in U.S.A.

CHAPTER ONE

THE Yorkshire hills rose majestically over the shimmering vast waters of Lake Rannaleigh, their towering peaks already lost in the cold grey mists that were rolling slowly down over the rugged russet-brown hills. Megan Parkinson released the pressure on the accelerator without even being aware of her action, her heart twisting with a sudden sharp pain at the sight of the well-remembered scene. The car slowed down to a virtual stop and Megan allowed herself a moment of uncharacteristic self-indulgence. A ghost of a smile flickered over her face as her expressive green eyes softened with sentimental tears.

Everything was just as she remembered it: the tiny square, the two small hotels, happily co-existing, sharing the steady flow of tourists, and Mrs Bain's name was still painted in bold black capital letters across the top of the corner shop. It sold absolutely anything anyone could ever need, as well as being the only post office for miles around. Megan remembered it all affectionately, a gentle sigh escaping from her softly parted lips.

Her eyes clouded momentarily with sudden doubts as too many memories flooded into her mind, disturbing her snatched moment of tranquillity. She bit nervously, her teeth sinking tenderly into her full bottom lip as all her nerves tensed uneasily. She cast a quick, protective glance over her shoulder at the innocently sleeping form curled up on the rear seat. He looked surprisingly fragile in repose. His delicate features took on a fragile quality that denied his physical strength and determined character, which were only recently was becoming a problem for her.

An instinctive smile tugged at the corners of her mouth, curling her full lips as she looked at him. The metamorphosis had already started; he was beginning to look more and more like his father with each passing day. Megan wondered whether she was just over-sensitive to his looks, searching for resemblances, a part of her hoping that he would look like his father. Though the thought caused equal amounts of pain and pleasure to her, Megan knew she had no control over the situation. Her expression softened as she reached out and tucked the car-rug around her son's unprotected shoulders.

At that moment the bright glare of headlights flashed at her, causing her to blink rapidly. She jumped as a car overtook her, its horn blaring at her obstruction. She caught a glimpse of the hard profile of the driver's handsome face as he sped past. Her head spun round, drawn by the familiar visage, her heart contracting violently within her. Megan stared after the car, all the old pain resurfacing with a cruel vengeance. Her eyes remained fixed on the rear lights, as if trapped by their brightness, till they were tiny pin-pricks of red fading into the distance.

'It couldn't have been him,' she said aloud to herself. 'Not here, not now.' She felt her teeth clamp against each other as she ground the words through her clenched mouth and struggled to contain the rise of panic that was surging through her trembling body. It was her mind playing tricks, she told herself, trying to remain calm as her heart began to thud painfully against her tight chest.

Just coming back here was enough to stir up so many hidden ghosts and bitter memories.

The frown deepened across Megan's brow as she questioned the wisdom of returning, but circumstances beyond her control had forced her return, she remembered with a painful twist of her heart.

Much to her regret, Megan hadn't been able to come back for her mother's funeral. Her death had been so sudden—a traffic accident—and Luke had still been in hospital, undergoing a series of tests while doctors sought the cause of his illness, and she couldn't leave him. He had been much too ill and frightened. She hoped her mother would have understood, but she doubted whether the rest of the community had. She could imagine the scandal her absence had caused and shook her head. She had been forced to leave Rannaleigh all those years ago to avoid scandal. She knew that the past would never stop haunting her but surely, she kept reassuring herself, that driver could not possibly have been him? Not Darrow Maine.

She resumed her journey, but that fleeting glimpse only served to remind her of the gamble she had taken in coming back. A bitter smile twisted her mouth. Maybe nothing here had changed but she had. She had left here a broken-hearted young girl, but she was returning a fully mature woman, with a rapidly growing son. But had her heart ever really mended? a taunting whisper mocked her. Wasn't part of her still a young girl, longing for her past, so that she imagined that Darrow Maine had just driven past her? Megan shook her head in an attempt to shake the doubts that niggled in the back of her mind.

Dusk was falling as she parked the car outside the reception area. The sky was a water-colour grey and a cold moon was already hanging in the sky like a huge silver coin. Megan closed the car door quietly, so as not to wake her precious child. She shivered. There was an icy nip in the evening air and her warm breath made clouds in the dusky light. She pulled her cashmere coat closer around her, its thick collar reaching up to her ears as she strode over the car park, her feet crunching on the gravel path. A smile of satisfaction touched her lips at the unstated elegance of the interior. At least she had returned home in style, she mused, wondering how long it would take for word to get round that she was back.

Megan smiled warmly as she reached out for the keys to her lakeside lodge, eager to settle in, but her smile froze, her breath stolen painfully from her as the searing shock of recognition swept over her. It was Darrow.

She was barely aware of the weight of the keys as the receptionist dropped them heavily into her outstretched palm, though instinctively her fingers closed tightly around the cold metal, glad of the feel of something solid as her whole world seemed to come crashing down around her. She was no longer listening to the hotel receptionist; all her senses were trained on the silent, menacing figure that had suddenly appeared behind her.

She stiffened in absolute dread as his cold, dark eyes fixed on her with an electrifying intensity. She felt her breath catch in her tightening chest as she faced him. His hard, icy gaze sent a shiver of apprehension through her body. It was so unlike him. He was a completely changed man, cold and aloof.

Had she fooled herself for all these years? she questioned herself silently. Had she held on to an image that had been self-created, a dream of a man who had only ever existed in her foolish young mind? She had clearly remembered those eyes as soft and gentle, holding a shining light of loving warmth touched with a wicked gleam that mirrored his zest for life. Now they were like freezing shards of ice, cruel and ruthless. Megan shut her eyes momentarily, to block out the image she now saw, a mockery of the man she had known.

She dragged her eyes from his hard, hypnotic gaze and concentrated on the receptionist, forcing herself to appear calm though her mind was a riot of emotions and thoughts. She never would have come back if she had known he was here. It was painful enough having to return, to rake up all the old memories, without the added problem of him being here. She smiled politely as she took the sheaf of papers being handed to her, nodding in agreement as she moved back, eager to be away from him. She could still feel his icy blue eyes searing into the very depths of her soul, as if searching for some trace of the girl he had known. Megan's eyes darted quickly back to his but she could detect no glimmer of recognition, and, despite everything, that hurt.

'Megan.' His low voice was unmistakable, its deep and resonant tone instantly recognisable. She felt the panic rise in her chest as a fleeting shiver of expectation. Yet gone was the familiar intimacy she remembered; there was only a trace of bitter humour in his tone. She turned, her expression questioning, though her blood had chilled to freezing within her. Her agitation was growing with every passing minute as she met the cool appraisal of his eyes.

'Yes?' she said politely, her voice betraying none of her inner turmoil as she caught the familiar scent of his aftershave that teased half-forgotten secrets back into her mind. His eyebrows rose swiftly, as if he was amused by her cool façade. 'Can I help you?' Megan asked, keeping her voice distinctly polite as she looked at him, disturbed by the changes she saw there.

There was a strain to his expression, a sharpness to his handsome features that had not been there before, but his mouth was as sensuous as ever, still full of the heady promise of love—love that she had given so willingly and foolishly. Megan tried to suffocate the growing resentment she felt at his presence and the threat it posed. It had been difficult enough to come back, especially under the circumstances, without him being here to exacerbate the situation.

'It's been a long time, Megan,' he commented drily, ignoring her question as his eyes travelled quickly over her body with an intensity that heated her blood. She stiffened slightly under his deliberate scrutiny, hating the effect that his close proximity was having on her, and she forced her body to relax, casually flicking her red hair from her face.

'Thirteen years is a long time, Darrow,' she agreed, her voice unexpectedly composed, carefully hiding the confusion that raged beneath her cool exterior.

He nodded slowly in agreement, a frown creasing hi' brow. 'You've changed,' he noted, nodding apprecia' tively.

Megan allowed herself a secret smile. She certainly carried the veneer of confidence well. The skilfully applied make-up and expensive clothes all helped to create the image of a confident, outgoing woman, but inside she was still the little girl searching for the love and security that she had never really known, and which she was determined to give her own son. A sudden wave of panic surged through her body as she thought of the damage Darrow's presence could have on Luke.

'I'll take that as a compliment,' she said serenely, pushing her fears to the back of her mind. 'Shall I?' she added, her veneer slipping under his intense scrutiny.

'Yes,' he replied, his eyes never leaving her face, and she felt a touch of heat colour her cheeks.

'You're looking well,' she returned, hating this banal conversation, but she was at a complete loss as to what to say under the circumstances. He did look well, too, she mused. The years had only added to his strength of character. His body was as firm and lean as ever, but he had always enjoyed sports of all kinds—a real outdoor man, she remembered with painful clarity. 'Older, perhaps,' she finally acknowledged, fixing a smile on her face.

'None of us is getting any younger,' he agreed with a smile, then added seriously, 'And yet there was a time when we couldn't wait to be older, remember?'

Remember? How could she ever forget, when she carried with her the constant symbol of their love? It had been love—at least then. Until he had gone to America and fallen in love with someone else, all in a matter of a few months. They had loved each other deeply and that was the reason why she had never told him. She had not wanted to stand in his way.

A grey veil of unshed tears filmed her eyes as her mind drifted back to that fateful day. It hadn't been a deliberate ploy, but once she had found herself pregnant, Megan had thought that no one would stop them marrying. She had longed to tell Darrow, to see the pleasure on his face when she told him the wonderful news.

But he had had news of his own, she remembered with pain. A chance of a lifetime. He had won a writing scholarship—a year in America. She couldn't have told him, robbed him of his chance to become a writer, stood in the way of his ambition. She had known how much that meant to him, and besides, he'd be back, so she had foolishly thought.

'Some of us grew up very quickly anyway,' she said

with sudden bitterness as she recalled how he had betrayed her.

At first he had kept in touch. Letters had arrived three or four times a week, and Carrie had been mentioned in every one. Then nothing for one whole month, not a line, and she had known. She had understood what had happened.

He had mentioned Carrie, a girl he had met, in all his previous letters and they had obviously been seeing a lot of each other. Megan had known that she couldn't compete with an attractive American who had wealth and position while she had nothing to offer to him—and how that had hurt. The pain of separation had been almost unbearable, but the realisation that she had lost him forever had seared her very soul.

She watched him stiffen now at the sharpness of her voice and it gave her a grim pleasure. 'I was glad to get away,' she added, throwing at him a final insult, reminding him that she too had found someone else even if her relationship with Karl had only been a fiction to save her pride. She was delighted when she saw that it irritated him.

'So why come back now?' he questioned. There was a trace of hidden anger in his tone, an unspoken accusation that he was unable to make. Megan felt a sudden surge of anger through her body but she quickly masked it. She had to remain as cool and as distant as he. She would never, ever give him the satisfaction of seeing her respond to him, no matter how difficult that might be.

'My mother—' she began simply, but he cut in, embarrassed by his own insensitivity.

'I forgot, I'm sorry, Megan,' he reassured her, for a fleeting moment looking like the young man she had known, so that the ice around her heart melted a little, warmed by his sympathy. He pushed his thick dark hair from his face, revealing an attractive touch of grey to his temples, a sad reminder that time had indeed travelled on, forcing an unbridgeable chasm between them.

She remembered that hair, falling gently between her eager fingers, soft and warm, and a faint tint of colour rose to her face at the memory which sprang so easily to mind. She promptly tried to dismiss it, struggling to return her thoughts to more neutral ground. She smiled briefly as their eyes met and held with the strong tie of the past. She dropped her head, turning away, knowing that he had seen the misting of her eyes in memory of what might have been. They had been so young, so in love...

The years they had been apart seemed to vanish as Megan's mind drifted back to those heady, magical days when everything had seemed so perfect.

Darrow, despite everyone else's doubts, had kept in touch with Megan the whole time he was at university, but the separation caused by his year in America had proved his love for her was not strong enough. He had found someone else and abandoned her—not that she would ever have let him know that. Her pride wouldn't have let her. She had played him at his own game. She had exaggerated her friendship with Karl, the attractive German hitch-hiker who had been taking a walking holiday in the Yorkshire dales and had stayed for the rest of the summer, doing casual work at the local boat-yard.

'Megan,' he said huskily, moving closer, taking full advantage of her momentary lapse. A shudder of anguish tore through her body and she raised her hands before her, to prevent him from touching her. Megan knew her barriers would never be strong enough to cope with his touch.

She was already too vulnerable, weakened by the flood of emotions that were sweeping over her. It had been such a difficult year. Luke had been stricken by a general malaise that had baffled doctors for a time before their diagnosis of glandular fever. Then there had been her mother's sudden death, and now her return home, after all those years of being away.

'Don't,' she ordered, but her voice was weak and it sounded more like a desperate plea, whispered in hope. 'Darrow, my mother's death…coming back here…' Her voice trailed off as his strong fingers curled around her wrists, drawing her hands down. His impetuous action caught her off guard, and the impact of the sudden warm touch on her skin riveted her to the spot.

'Why not? Why have you come back?' he demanded hoarsely. 'You knew I was here. Didn't you…?' His tone had taken on a steely edge and his grip had intensified, forcing an immediate denial from Megan. Her eyes darted to his, searching his face for compassion but finding none, and his question troubled her; what did he think she had come back for? She struggled fruitlessly against his stubborn strength.

'No, you're wrong; I had no idea,' Megan protested, alarmed by the thunderous clouds that swirled in the darkest depths of his eyes. She tried to pull away but her actions were futile; he was far too strong for her and her reaction only served to fuel his temper.

'Then why now?' he derided with a cruel sneer, the contempt etched clearly on his ruthless face, pulling her closer till their bodies almost touched. Megan tensed every fibre of her body as the haunting aroma of his aftershave teased her nostrils, flooding her with agonising memories.

'I've told you—I'm here to sort out my mother's estate,' protested Megan, confronting his anger with complete candour, and she saw the flickering realisation in his eyes as he released her, his anger suddenly appeased. For a split-second she had seen the cool mask of indifference fall away and she stepped back in confusion.

'Of course. I'm so sorry about your mother.' His voice was now smooth and good-tempered, as if his outburst had never happened, which increased Megan's confusion still further.

'Don't be,' Megan replied quickly, as eager as him to put the strange incident behind her. 'We never really got on, were never that close,' she confessed, without a trace of remorse. She had come to accept their differences a long time ago.

It had been partly her mother's fault that she had had to leave Rannaleigh; they would have never agreed about the situation. She had always been far too conventional for her mother, a disappointment in so many ways, yet they had kept in contact, grown closer over the years. Her mother, who had doted on her grandson, had made numerous visits to London, but Megan had never felt comfortable with the idea of going back to Rannaleigh, and by then her mother had understood her reasons and supported them. It was one of the few things they had come to agree on. Megan's mother had respected her daughter's independence. It had been the one thing they had in common besides their love for Luke.

Darrow remained silent, his expression fathomless, his dark eyes brooding.

'I couldn't make the funeral,' she explained painfully, filling in the silence that only seemed to increase the tension between them. 'But I've come now,' she added lightly, her features impassive, displaying none of her inner hurt. But he caught the note of tension in her voice and his lips parted into an understanding smile. Megan dropped her own gaze, unable to bear the compassion in the shining eyes.

'She was a strong individual, your mother,' he said graciously. 'Unfortunately she expected the same from everyone else,' he concluded, a grimness entering his tone, and Megan knew he was remembering the painful scenes between herself and her mother which he had been an unwilling spectator to.

She felt her cheeks grow hot as a vivid flash of those adolescent arguments flashed through her mind. Yet, despite everything, in the end her mother had been right. Darrow was not to be trusted. Megan had been forced to admit it. They *had* been too young to be truly in love and when Darrow's love had been tested he had failed her so spectacularly that she still remembered the twist of the knife searing her heart.

'Are you planning on staying?' His eyes narrowed on her face and she wondered where his source of annoyance was coming from. Surely she was the injured party, not him, and she felt a justifiable anger niggle inside her, deep down in the hidden well of emotions that she knew would belong forever to her first love.

'I don't know,' she answered truthfully. Until that moment she had thought of it only as a passing visit; now her heart seemed to be aching to stay. 'I don't think so.'

She desperately scanned his face, but found nothing to encourage her to change her mind. She swallowed the painful lump that caught in her throat at the realisation that she had hoped to find some trace of affection. 'There's nothing for me here. There never was,' she added, a trace of bitterness entering her tone, and her eyes met his in silent confirmation.

'Wasn't there?' he snapped tautly. His anger was now

well under control, but Megan could see the signs of its brittleness. His eyes had darkened into swirling inky pools of molten fierceness that betrayed his growing fury.

'It was all such a long time ago, Darrow.' She looked away as she shook her head, hating the sense of betrayal that was resurfacing after all this time. 'I have to go. Excuse me.' She flicked an anxious glance towards the door, suddenly agitated.

'Wait,' he ordered, his arm outstretched to prevent her moving. 'I want to talk to you.' His look was hard and demanding, his tone honed with the sharp steel edge of command.

Megan froze, responding instinctively to the authority in his tone, then hated herself for her weakness. She was no longer the silly girl he had known, susceptible to his overpowering strength.

'There's nothing to say,' Megan snapped back, suddenly fearful. She couldn't afford to be alone with him. How long could she trust herself in his company without the past coming back to haunt them? They were strangers now, she inwardly argued, despite the disturbing effect he was having on her. What do I know of him? He must have changed. Have I? she mused desperately.

'I think there is.'

Megan gasped as she fought to save her breath, suddenly fearful, and without being aware of her action her eyes flew quickly to the door as an icy grip tightened around her heart. She knew she could not afford the luxury of basking in the past. There was her son to consider.

Yet even now, after all these years, and though she felt her defences weakening against him, she knew it was not only herself she had to protect from this dangerous man. She moved slightly away, carefully surrounding herself in a protective layer that she hoped he would find im-

pregnable. His smouldering eyes held her trapped, and
Megan tried to pull away as she felt her pathetic barriers
begin to melt.

'Have dinner with me tonight?' he asked gruffly, his
tone full of tension, a pulse throbbing in the strong line
of his jaw. 'Here in the hotel,' he added quickly, seeing
the refusal already present in her eyes.

'No,' she objected, too quickly, betraying her fear, her
eyes straying to the door as she thought of Luke. He
seized on her fear with characteristic aggression, a smile
of victory already curling his sensuous mouth, revealing
a set of perfect white teeth.

'For old times' sake,' he crooned, his voice dangerously soft and a hidden invitation swirling in the slumberous depths of his hypnotic eyes. Megan nearly weakened, drowning all her doubts in the familiar glow of his
heated gaze, her own eyes softening in response. 'It's the
least you owe me.'

Steel had entered his voice, a harshness she had not
expected, and her eyes leapt to his face, troubled by his
words. But the freezing look of contempt that glistened
in the icy depths of his eyes prevented her from speaking.
She frantically searched his face, looking for a glimpse
of the man she had once known.

'Well, Meggie?' he taunted, using her familiar pet
name to weaken her still further. He had sensed her distrust and was playing on it, his eyes shining now with
teasing laughter, and in that brief moment she caught a
sudden flash of the man she had once known and loved.
He reached out, placing his hand on her shoulder, and
Megan's stomach twirled with an instinctive excitement
at the impact his unexpected touch had on her. And in
that transient moment she might have weakened, but the
door suddenly swung open.

An icy draught of cold air blasted towards them, chilling the warmth that had begun to grow between them. They both turned simultaneously to see a tousled-haired youngster with a harsh look of resentment on his face. He fixed his cold eyes on the pair of them, his disapproval at their close proximity apparent in his narrowing eyes and mounting frown.

For a moment he said nothing. His stare flicked quickly to Darrow, making a swift but comprehensive inventory of him, before he turned his attention back on to Megan. A look of scorn flickered across his face and he raised his eyebrows in mockery.

'You've been ages,' he said sullenly, directing his accusation at Megan and deliberately cutting out Darrow's presence.

'I'm sorry,' Megan stated briefly, annoyed by his obvious rudeness. 'I thought you were asleep,' she concluded, casting an anxious covert glance at Darrow to see his reaction to her child. His eyes shone with curiosity, a quizzical expression on his face as he studied him with deep interest.

'I woke up.' It was a bald statement accompanied by another look of resentment, the dark brows drawing together over the glitter of frustration in his eyes.

'Obviously,' agreed Megan, calmly looking at her son who over the past few months had seemed to be slowly changing into a total stranger. His glandular fever hadn't helped; it had left him a little weak, and Megan knew she was being over-protective but she couldn't help herself, despite the resentment it caused in Luke. She was so frightened of the thought of losing him, just as she had lost his father, that she was totally confused as to how she should behave.

They had always been so close, him so caring and

gentle, but now he was sometimes rude and often distant.
A typical teenager, Megan tried to reassure herself, but
his behaviour still hurt more deeply than she cared to
admit. This chance of a holiday was just what they both
needed to re-establish their bond. They faced each other
now, an improbable discomfort widening the chasm that
was beginning to develop between them. The deadly lull
only added to the already tense atmosphere as the three
of them stayed locked each in their own inner turmoil.

Megan was aware of the stiffening of Darrow beside
her as he purposefully fixed his whole attention on Luke.
Luke held his gaze with equal hostility and Darrow's lips
twisted as Luke continued to stare at him stubbornly with
cold contempt. Megan found herself struggling to subdue
a hysterical bubble of laughter that was growing with
every passing moment. It was ironic for father and son
to stand so close, watching each other with such deep
interest, and be unaware of their relationship.

'Are you coming now?' demanded Luke, already turning to leave. Megan moved forward, following him anxiously. She desperately wanted to keep them well away
from each other but Darrow's arm shot out, gripping her
tightly around the upper arm. His iron hold warned her
that his formidable temper was about to erupt. Meggie's
head swirled around, her heart already thudding out a
death-knell as she confronted the black darkness that
filled his eyes. Had he realised the truth? she thought
suddenly, feeling sick.

'Who's he?' he bit out, the words sounding like a hiss
as they escaped through his clenched teeth.

The furious tone of his voice seared through her body
till every nerve tingled with foreboding, her mouth suddenly went dry and she flicked her tongue nervously over
her lips. Her mind went blank. She stood rooted to the

spot, her face draining of all colour as she faced the dark fury that was building with every passing moment. She could hear the frantic hammering of her heart against her tightening ribcage.

'He's my son,' she managed at last, though her voice was a thin whisper of despair. His grip tightened at her words but he remained absolutely silent, his body rigid with tension. Megan knew he was fighting some inner doubt and she waited, mentally praying for her escape.

'I didn't know you had a child.' His voice was a harsh whisper, as if some sharp pain was trapped in his throat. Megan looked at him anxiously, her whole body trembling as she watched his gaze switch swiftly back to Luke, staring at him with an intensity that unnerved her. She silently prayed over and over again that soon she would be free. The last thing she wanted was for Luke to find out the truth. Their relationship was already on thin ice at the moment. She had only recently heard the painful longing in his voice when he spoke of the father he had never known.

'And the father?' he drawled, his eyes darting back to hers and fixing on her with an icy intent. Megan felt a flush of colour to her face as she struggled to keep her emotions under control. She normally deftly avoided any questions, but she knew Darrow would not be so easily swayed.

'Karl Meyer, my husband,' she retorted, her voice growing stronger as she trotted out the well-worn lie. A lie she had been forced to invent to protect herself and her son against the pain of his rejection. Darrow's eyebrow's lifted slightly, his mouth thinning to an angry line.

'And where's Karl now?' he demanded, the self-assurance in his voice irritating her more than she was willing to admit, even to herself.

'My husband died several years ago,' Megan replied frostily, hating the intrusion into her private life. He had given up his rights to that with his betrayal.

'And he is your only child?' he asked, a tightness in his voice as he looked deep into her eyes, and Megan quickly lowered her long lashes over her eyes to prevent him from seeing the truth that she knew she would be unable to hide from him.

'Yes.' Megan forced a smile, though her insides were churning with despair. Was he jealous or merely curious? she wondered, a sudden ache piercing her heart.

'He doesn't look like you...'

'No,' snapped Megan quickly. 'He takes after his father.' Her eyes couldn't quite meet his as she replied.

'Are you coming?' Luke's voice was sharp as he turned back, glaring at them both with obvious disapproval. Megan gave an apologetic smile to Darrow, but he seemed unperturbed by Luke's rude outburst and strolled over to meet him. Luke watched his approach with caution, his face sulky, the silence only adding to the tense atmosphere. Darrow broke the silence with his customary ease, as if oblivious to the tension between the mother and her child.

'My name is Darrow,' he offered, his voice firm, full of authority. He stretched out his hand, his gesture more one of challenge than friendship, and Megan mentally prayed that Luke would respond. For a moment she thought her prayers had been wasted and her heart shrank within her as a sudden shaft of piercing pain seared through her. For a brief moment she thought her heart would break in two; just seeing them together held a bittersweet pain. 'I'm an old friend of your mother's,' he continued, taking Luke's hand in a firm grasp. 'I was trying to persuade her to have dinner with me this evening.'

'She can if she wants,' muttered Luke, trying to sound careless, yet suddenly he seemed so vulnerable to Megan and her heart went out to him. The mask of manhood that he tried so hard to wear often slipped.

'I had no idea she had to have your permission,' drawled Darrow, with a friendly smile, but it was not returned. Luke was unable to match Darrow and did not know how to respond.

Megan joined them, part of her wanting them to at least like each other. Her eyes darted frantically from Luke to Darrow, sensing their disapproval of one another, and her heart slowly sank within her. It had been a fleeting dream that they had both shattered.

'I knew Darrow a long time ago, Luke,' Megan explained breathlessly, the pain catching in her throat at the obvious antipathy. Luke nodded in acknowledgement but said nothing; his eyes were fixed on Darrow with deep interest and suspicion.

'Come on, we'd best get settled in,' cajoled Megan, tossing the keys in her hand in a carefree gesture that was far removed from her true feelings. She knew now that her return was on a disaster course, but she was powerless to do anything about it. She turned as she opened the door to allow Luke to leave, then she turned back to Darrow, and forced her voice to sound light, almost friendly.

'It was nice to see you again, Darrow.' Her cool tone did not betray the turmoil of emotions that were twirling around inside. 'Perhaps we'll meet again some time,' she added, confident that she would not see him again, and yet that caused a sharp pain deep down inside.

Darrow's mouth widened into a perfect smile, triumph

curling the corners of his sensuous mouth as he viewed
Megan with a cool air of superiority. Megan shuddered
as her eyes rose to his, trying to fathom where his amusement came from and not trusting him an inch. She knew
him too well to be fooled by his casual stance. His hand
rested on the door-handle, opening it still wider to allow
her to leave.

'No doubt we will,' he agreed, in a smoky voice that
put Megan on edge, every nerve in her body suddenly
alerted to some hidden danger.

'What do you mean?' she breathed raggedly, hating
the storm of emotion that was sweeping through her
body. His smile twisted in cruelty and his eyebrows rose
in mockery; a rumble of laughter sounded deep in his
chest.

'You mean you really don't know?' he asked in disbelief, the mocking light in his eyes holding her trapped,
unable to move.

'Know? Know what?' demanded Megan, a spiral of
fear twisting up her spine and a cold dread seeping over
her trembling frame.

Darrow inclined his head backwards. 'This is mine—
my hotel, my complex.' The cold, proud possession in
his voice confirmed what he was saying, and Megan
gasped in horror.

'Yours?' she whispered in disbelief, hoping for a denial and yet already knowing it was the truth. Her heart
shrank within her. She had been such a fool, allowing
the travel agent to make all the arrangements. She would
have certainly noticed the name of the proprietor, and
never would even have dreamt of coming here, and now
it was too late. She knew there was little chance of accommodation anywhere else in peak season, and besides,

she didn't want to give him the impression that his presence made any difference to her.

'Yes, Megan, mine,' he replied in a controlled voice, but Megan could see the malice in the depths of his ruthless eyes. 'I told you I'd make it one day.' The coldness of his attitude frightened her; his face had become distorted with anger and hate. 'It's a pity you couldn't have kept your promise and waited for me,' he snarled, the bitter rage spilling out, and Megan flinched at the anger in his tone.

She felt her anger flare up inside her and she tried hard to control her temper. Her fists tightened into balls of rage as she glared back at him, unable to comprehend the injustice of his remark. 'I'm so pleased you've been successful,' she admitted, resenting the sacrifices she had made to make him a success.

'Are you?' he mocked, his expression challenging, but his voice was flat.

'Of course I am,' she said with forced brightness, as a sharp pain of regret fleetingly touched her deeply, and yet it was the truth. It made it all worthwhile. It justified her deceit, vanquished any last doubts she had had. All the lies, her struggles, the loneliness of her life now made sense, and yet a sting of bitterness cut into her as she remembered all the hardships she had faced alone just so he could fulfil his ambition.

He had always been ambitious; Rannaleigh had never seemed big enough to contain him. He had loved the idea of America—the size, the challenge, the thought of being a success in a big way through his writing. Megan had known that until he tried he would never be satisfied, so she had given him his freedom, expecting his return, but then she had lost him forever to someone else.

'You don't look it.' Darrow noted, inclining his head

closer to hers so he could get an even clearer view of her troubled expression.

'I'm sorry, I was thinking of something else,' Megan confessed, her mind coming back to the present with difficulty as the familiar smell of his aftershave filled her senses. His dark eyes fixed on her, studying her closely for a moment.

'Thinking what a foolish mistake you made running off and marrying someone else instead of waiting for me?' he jeered cruelly, seeming oblivious to the sorrow growing in her misty eyes.

Megan reached out and touched his arm. The smooth cloth of his expensive suit could not hide the hard ripple of tension that ran the length of his arm. 'It wasn't like that...' she protested, shocked by the cruelty of his words.

'Wasn't it?'

'Darrow, please...' she began, suddenly wanting to explain, regardless of his reaction and despite the terrible repercussions it would cause in her own life.

He pulled back, his body as tense as an over-strung violin, and with a harsh expression that barely concealed how much he despised her. His face was set in sharp, rigid lines, grim and furious, and his eyes were as black and as bitter as over-stewed coffee.

Megan stepped back, fearful of the anger and hate that crackled beneath his thin veneer of control.

'Darrow, please,' he mocked back, imitating her voice roughly. 'The truth hurts, does it?' he sneered, allowing her to feel the weight of his full contempt.

'Truth? Truth?' she repeated, matching his anger with her own. 'What would you know of truth?' she flung back at him.

Megan pulled away from him and rushed out of the door, hot, salty tears splashing down her face at the injustice of it all. She knew she shouldn't have come back.

CHAPTER TWO

MEGAN rubbed the back of her hand over her face in an attempt to erase the sorrow from her face. She couldn't allow Luke to see her distress. He was far too astute and was bound to question her until she told him the whole story, and that she could never do. It would be a total betrayal of their lives together.

'Who's he?' Luke snapped as she slid into the car beside him, shoving the papers from the receptionist on to his lap and starting the engine immediately.

'Darrow Maine,' Megan answered abruptly, a rasp burning the back of her throat as she struggled to keep her emotions under control. 'An old friend,' she added, hopeful that that piece of information would be all he required.

'I see,' he mumbled, too engrossed in the papers to notice the fearful glance his mother flicked to him as she caught the undercurrent in his tone. Megan felt herself forced to say more. It was inevitable that they would bump into Darrow and she wanted their meetings to be as uneventful as possible.

'He owns the hotel and complex,' she explained as she craned her neck to see the names that were painted on small posts along the roadside. She carefully steered the car into the space next to their lodge, flicking off the engine with a weary sigh.

'Does he?' Luke asked with interest as he opened the car door. 'He must be loaded.'

'Does everything nowadays have to be valued on monetary worth?' Megan retorted, exasperated by her son's apparent obsession with material wealth and desperately wondering if she had failed him in some way. They seemed slowly to be drifting apart, and Megan was determined to stop the slow deterioration of their relationship. She had struggled too hard for too long on her own to let it just fade away. It had been one long struggle bringing up a child alone, trying to make ends meet on the meagre amount she managed to earn. She pulled their luggage from the boot, offering him the cases which he accepted with a grin.

'What other type of value is there?' he asked, ducking as Megan took a friendly swoop at his head. 'Come on we'd best unpack something, even if it's only something for tonight.' He laughed as Megan locked the car.

'Tonight?' Megan asked, a frisson of alarm racing down her spine as she caught the excitement in his tone.

'Yes, had you not been so engrossed in conversation you would have seen the posters,' he informed her as they entered their lodge. He dropped the luggage immediately, racing over to the patio doors and pulling them open with enthusiasm. 'Hey, get a look at this view,' he called, his eyes scanning over the flat mirror of water and the range of mountains that rose up as a backdrop.

'What posters?' Megan asked anxiously as she joined him on the patio, leaning on the wall and soaking in the beautiful scene that eased her troubled soul. She wrapped a protective arm over his shoulders and he leant against her.

Megan's heart filled with emotion. This holiday was so important after the strain of this last year. It was a chance for them to be together again without the distractions of work, and Megan was determined that it would help to heal the rift that was growing between them. He needed to build up his confidence again as it had taken such a bad knock since his illness.

'It's all there.' Luke jerked his head to the disarray of papers that he had dropped to the floor, scattering them everywhere. 'Party-time starts at eight o'clock prompt, and I get the impression that Darrow Maine would not like to be kept waiting,' he concluded, moving back into the large lounge with Megan following with a sinking heart.

'You want to go, do you?' she asked, forcing a brighter tone into her voice and suffocating her sense of desperation. She picked up the papers and pushed them back into a neat pile, her heart already thudding out a death-knell at his anticipated answer.

'Dead right I do,' he answered quickly. 'They're going to tell us what's on offer and I want to know,' he said, snatching up his own cases. 'It's about time I took up sport seriously again. I'm not even on the first team any more. Don't you want to go?' he asked, stopping to await her answer. A frown of disappointment was forming over his bright eyes.

'Of course,' she replied brightly, flashing him a smile and forcing her personal doubts from her mind. She couldn't bear to disappoint Luke. They depended on one another so much, their relationship all the more intense because they had only ever had each other. Megan had had a couple of boyfriends, but no one could ever match Darrow or come between her and Luke. This was their holiday, a much deserved rest, and she knew how much he wanted to get back on the school's first team, and no one, not even Darrow Maine, was going to spoil her chance of that.

*   *   *

Megan's eyes quickly darted around the room. It was filled with a mixture of people, young and old, sporty types and the more sedate, but thankfully there was no trace of Darrow. She sank gratefully into a Victorian tub chair that had been carefully restored and reupholstered in a tartan fabric that matched the heavy curtains and swags decorating the expansive windows which gave a unique view of the rolling hills and the lake below. Luke had disappeared immediately after collecting her a glass of the delicate sparkling wine that was being offered to all guests.

'I've just found a fantastic computer-room,' he said, rushing back with a wicked grin, and Megan raised her eyebrows in despair. There was little chance of seeing him again for some time, she thought, taking a sip of her wine and nodding her approval as he disappeared again.

'Can I tempt you?' Darrow raised an oval platter of canapés towards Megan, taking her by surprise. Her heart thudded rapidly before settling back into a steady rhythm.

'I'd love one,' she agreed, suddenly feeling hungry and delighting in the selection she was being offered. 'I had no idea you acted as waiter as well,' she joked lightly, sensing that his gesture was meant as an attempt at good-will.

'I don't normally, but I thought I would make an exception in your case.' His voice was low and warm and she treasured the sound of it. Megan glanced up and his dark eyes held her.

'Why?'

'I'm sorry about before. It just came as a shock—you, married.'

'I did write and tell you I was considering Karl's proposal,' she replied lightly. She had hoped for a different response but he had not even bothered to reply to her letter, which had only served to confirm her fears that he had found someone else.

'And with a son,' he continued, unaware of her words. His smile faded slightly and a cold chill swept over her, but she nodded, trying to simplify the hundreds of questions that churned over and over in her mind. She tilted back her chin, not wanting to give the impression that she cared.

'You never married, then?' she asked.

Her heart skipped a beat as she waited for his answer, preparing to hear for herself the confirmation that he had betrayed their love.

'Never.'

It wasn't the answer she had expected. It was like a sharp slap in the face and shock was quickly replaced by anger.

'Not married!' she exclaimed, more angry with herself than him. It was so unfair.

'I nearly took the plunge,' he said calmly, unaware of the searing, heated anger that tore through her body. All her noble sacrifices had been a waste, she thought. She was just the first, no doubt, in a long line of foolish women who had thought he was capable of commitment. She tried vainly to appear indifferent to this revelation but she was burning with curiosity and fury. She had been told by his mother, Janet, that he was having a serious relationship. She had told her clearly that marriage was round the corner, and Megan hadn't had the confidence to question her. She'd felt so foolish. Megan recalled how she had feigned indifference to the news although her heart had been breaking. Had it all been lies? She had to know.

'Cold feet?' She tried to keep her voice light and joky,

but she had been a victim of *his* sense of humour and
her amusement was hollow. He shrugged.

'In a way. I just realised it would have been a mistake,
so I called it off.'

'I see.'

Megan didn't want to probe any deeper. For some reason the thought of him caring for someone else hurt her
more deeply than she was prepared to admit, even to
herself.

'Your marriage was happy?' he commented, his voice
strained but cool, and Megan felt the familiar panic that
rose in her chest whenever her marriage was mentioned.
She kept her lids lowered over her startled eyes to prevent
him from seeing the truth she knew would be shining
there.

'Yes, very,' she told him, hoping, for some reason, that
he would be hurt by her words. As she cast a covert
glance at his face she saw a flicker of emotion there, but
she knew it was pure fantasy to imagine it was jealousy.

'It must have been very hard to lose someone you
loved,' he said, with such deep understanding that Megan
felt a momentary guilt at her deceit.

'It was,' she admitted truthfully, but it was not Karl
she was thinking of.

'How did your son react?' he asked, his voice strangely
soft and soothing, and Megan glanced up, surprised by
his interest.

'He never knew his father,' she said quickly, her eyes
darting to his. It wasn't a lie. She would do everything
in her power to ensure that Luke never knew the truth.
It would be far too painful for both of them. Megan had
never told Luke that Karl was his father—it was one lie
she had known she couldn't live with—but she had not
denied it either. Luke had grown up with the idea that

his father was dead, and though Megan had longed to tell the truth she was afraid of the emotional damage it might cause.

'He doesn't look like you. Does he take after his father?' he asked, picking up a tiny, delicate blini topped with smoked salmon. It was a casual enough question, but Megan cursed the emotion his query was stirring within her.

'As he grows older, he looks more like his father,' she confessed.

She wanted to tell him about his son, longed to tell him, but she knew she couldn't. The web of lies she had carefully spun for Luke must remain intact. She would not allow her child to feel the pain of rejection she had been subjected to. He reached out, wrapping his strong, warm hand over hers, squeezing it gently.

'I'm sorry. It must be hard for you.'

'No, I'm just being silly,' she said quickly, fully aware of the heat from his hand that was slowly permeating her body. She felt her heart race at his familiar touch and she stared at his hand, looking at the dark mat of hairs that criss-crossed his hand with intensity. She was so sensitive to him that it frightened her. For once, after so many years, she felt alive again, every nerve in her body tingling with anticipation.

'My Meg, my poor Meg,' he crooned softly, stroking his slender fingers across her gently trembling hand. Her response was a soft, almost soundless laugh as she withdrew her hand from his. She was afraid of the sharp tug of attraction he was arousing in her and the intimate use of their childhood name for her.

'Poor!' She laughed hollowly. 'No, Darrow, my days of poverty are over.'

His eyes narrowed as he studied her, his expression hardening to granite.

'You're still poor Megan. You always will be till you learn true values.' He bit out the words, his anger spilling out in the bitter blue-blackness of his eyes.

'I know this, Darrow. It's easy to appreciate the finer things in life when you don't have to worry about the basics. I've struggled to achieve what I have now, and believe me there is no dignity in poverty. So don't preach to me about being poor in spirit till you have experienced it for yourself,' she threw back at him, hating his condescending attitude.

'What a change. I never saw you as a material girl,' he jeered, shocked by the change in her. 'I thought it odd that you were unable to make it to your mother's funeral. You're obviously able to come now. No doubt it was the will that brought you back.'

Megan was about to protest her innocence, but her words died on her lips. She could not reveal the real reason why she had missed the funeral as just then Luke returned.

'Hello, Luke. Did you win?' she asked, realising immediately that she did not have his attention.

'You do everything, don't you?' he asked Darrow with obvious enthusiasm. 'I've been talking to Suzie.' Megan saw the light of admiration glowing in her son's eyes and sighed inwardly. The last thing she needed was a bad case of hero-worship; the situation was difficult enough as it was.

'Whatever do you mean, Luke?' She laughed as he drew up a chair between them and picked up three different canapés, ignoring Megan's disapproving frown with customary ease. He popped two immediately in his mouth, nodding in approval and swallowing quickly in order to explain.

'River-rafting, abseiling, canoeing, skiing.' He paused to pick up another canapé and Megan gave his hand a sharp tap. Luke flashed Darrow a grin, and the easy bond that seemed to have sprung between them pierced Megan's heart.

'You don't mind, do you?' he asked, hardly waiting for Darrow to answer.

'No not all. Help yourself.'

Luke's grin broadened at his words; he was clearly delighting in the camaraderie.

'I'd love to try everything. Do you instruct, Mr...?'

'Darrow. Everyone calls me Darrow.'

'Darrow,' repeated Luke, enjoying the adult approach Darrow was taking with him. Megan twisted the stem of her wine glass, trying to remain indifferent to their close proximity and easy conversation. She watched them both with nervous expectation, a chill spiralling down her spine as she caught the close scrutiny Darrow was subjecting Luke to. His dark eyes were assessing Luke very closely indeed, and a tremor of apprehension vibrated through her body.

'Luke, fetch me another glass of wine, would you?' she asked. She had sounded abrupt and for a moment Luke looked confused, though he immediately responded by taking up her empty glass.

'I guess you two want to talk alone,' he said, making an exaggerated wink as he looked at Darrow, whose face broke out into a wide smile. Megan felt a warm flush of pink cover her cheeks and her eyes darted quickly from Luke to Darrow as a denial leapt swiftly to her lips.

'No, not at all.'

For a few moments after Luke had left silence fell between them. Megan glanced up, a wave of nausea seeping over her as she watched Darrow's eyes follow Luke's disappearing body. At last he had noticed, seen a trace of himself in the boy, and the thought flooded her with a mixture of feelings—delight and despair.

'I don't think he'll be able to do all the activities,' he informed her crisply, turning his attention back to her, and Megan immediately tensed. Afraid to look at him, Megan stared down at the table, stroking her fingers restlessly over a drip-mat.

'We are booked in for over a fortnight. Ample time, I would have thought...' she began, her voice strangely breathless as she awaited his condemnation of her keeping his son to herself.

'It wasn't the time factor I was referring to.'

There was a note of challenge in his voice that drew her gaze back to his, and his expression showed a smooth, worldly wisdom.

'Then what?' demanded Megan, suddenly defensive, her nerves tensing at his poker-faced expression which warned her that more was to come.

'He just doesn't look well enough,' he said matter-of-factly, but Megan sensed a criticism in his tone and her own feelings of insecurity immediately surfaced. She so desperately wanted him to be well. It was so very difficult being a one-parent family, trying hard to be both mother and father. She had tried to encourage him towards sporting activities but his enforced rest period had left him a little weaker than usual.

'Looks can be deceptive,' she retorted, angry with herself that he was evoking in her such a sense of overprotectiveness.

'I'm not suggesting he doesn't try some of the activities out, but—'

'I think I'm the best judge of what my son is capable of,' Megan cut in, furious by his lack of natural response to his own son, angered that he could not see himself mirrored in Luke's frame, waiting to grow into a strong, capable man.

'Oh, God, you're not one of those pushy mothers who insist on over-compensating for the lack of a father?' He grinned, unaware of the depth of pain he was causing her or how near the truth he might have touched.

'It's not a case of that. I just think you're making an incorrect judgement merely because of his looks,' she countered. The tone of conversation was swiftly changing to one of confrontation but she felt as if she was on a roller-coaster, thundering down a track, out of control.

'Don't be ridiculous. Why on earth should I do that?' he demanded, and Megan instantly tensed as his dark eyes narrowed on her. Megan felt her face redden as she realised that it was her own sensitivity to the situation that was causing the problem. She was reading far too much into his words.

'Look, I'm sure that Luke will be sensible enough to make his own choices,' she said briefly, hoping to draw a close over that line of conversation. She didn't want to talk about Luke; it was far too dangerous.

Darrow leant across the table, pushing to one side the half-empty platter of food in a gesture of annoyance. He flexed his shoulders as he drew closer and Megan again caught the teasing scent of his masculine aftershave.

'How old is he?' he snapped, staring across the table at her, his expression devoid of emotion.

Megan didn't answer—couldn't answer. She felt trapped, as if he had carefully laid the bait and like a fool

she had fallen for it. She could hear her heart thudding
painfully against her constricting chest and she dropped
her gaze, unable to confront the steel in his eyes.

'It doesn't matter,' he said airily, unaware of the huge
sigh of relief that silently escaped Megan's lips. 'The fact
remains that he has a dull complexion and his eyes look
heavy-lidded. He looks unwell…'

Megan's eyes flew to his, anger flaring in the cool
green.

'That's not a criticism, Megan, merely an observation,'
he countered immediately, seeing her reaction but refusing to acknowledge it fully. He still wanted to make his
point, regardless of how she felt about it. 'I was scrawny
myself at that age, but he looks tired and drawn,' he
admitted, which only served to twist the knife deeper into
her unhealed heart. 'To take on all the activities available
would be asking for trouble. One needs to build up stamina over a period of time.'

'I see,' Megan replied, too quickly, though she did
agree. She could see that what he was saying made sense
but she knew Luke's stubborn determination—a characteristic from his father, she mused. She was not prepared
to ruin her chances of strengthening their relationship by
refusing to allow him to do exactly what he wanted. It
still hurt more deeply than she wanted to admit that she
felt Luke was outgrowing her. Besides, she reassured herself, Luke was stronger than he appeared. Even the doctors had agreed with that, amazed at his quick recovery.

'Do you?' His voice was cold, cutting into her with
icy precision. 'I doubt that. You're fit and healthy, busy
running a health club, a sick child would hardly be an
ideal advertisement.'

'What do you mean by that?' Megan shot back.

'I think you've been either too busy to notice or deliberately blind to the fact...' he began to explain, his voice cold and detached.

'How dare you?' stormed Megan, her surprise matched only by her anger at his unfair remarks.

'I dare for this reason, Megan. I have a one hundred percent accident-free record here and I plan on keeping it that way,' he snarled, gripping her wrist in a painful clasp. 'I can't afford parents who refuse to see their own offspring's limitations, pushing them beyond their capabilities. It's dangerous and unforgivable.'

A wave of righteous indignation swept through Megan's body, heating her blood to boiling point. How dared he make assumptions about her and her relationship with Luke? He had no right, no right at all, she fumed inwardly, and yet knowing he did have some right only annoyed her even more.

'If you're suggesting that I'm pushing him you couldn't be more wrong. Luke wants to take part—he's very keen.'

'Is he? He looks worn out to me. An activity holiday is the last thing he needs. Rest and relaxation would do him more good. For God's sake, Megan, can't you see it?' he protested, fixing his eyes on her like a pair a darts.

'Luke's OK. He has a slim build but he's strong,' Megan countered, resenting his interference.

'You're blinkered, Megan. You refuse to see your son as he is,' he growled at her, furious at her obstinacy.

'I don't think you know Luke well enough to make any comment,' Megan told him in a glacier tone, the look on her face matching her icy voice.

'Don't be ridiculous, Megan,' he said dismissively, ignoring the expression on her face. 'Your ambition is blinding you. I'm sorry, but he's not going to live up to some bizarre ideal you have of him—he just hasn't your physical strength,' he told her firmly.

'Well, we'll just have to wait and see, won't we?' she retorted briskly, confident that Luke would show just how capable he was.

'There's no way I'm allowing him to over-stretch himself for your benefit. It could be extremely dangerous,' he told her, his tone brooking no argument and his jaw set firmly.

'Well, we wouldn't want anything upsetting your precious record, would we?' she goaded him, pain and frustration twisting her stomach. She paid no heed to the darkening of his eyes or the glitter of anger that flickered there. Like a wounded animal she just wanted to hit out, to hurt him as he was hurting her.

'You know damn well it's not a case of that...' he ground out, but his words faded as a shadow fell across the table. His anger evaporated immediately, to be replaced by a brilliant smile.

'Thanks, Luke,' he said, taking the glass and placing it in front of Megan, who was carefully avoiding his eyes. 'I think I'd best mix with some other guests,' Darrow went on, pushing himself away from the table and pausing for a moment, till Megan was forced to look up and confront his grim expression.

A frown marred Megan's usual smooth brow. She was annoyed at how smoothly he had managed to change his façade and direct his anger only at her.

'I'll see you later.' He smiled at both of them, but Megan could see another message clearly in his eyes, that warned her that he was determined to finish their talk.

'We'll be leaving shortly. We are both tired with the travelling,' Megan offered as an explanation, determined to go back to the safety of her cosy lodge.

His grin widened, showing a flash of white predatory teeth that made Megan inwardly wince.

'We have a dinner-date, don't we?'

'Come on, Mum,' agreed Luke. 'It's our first night. Besides, me and this lad from Manchester are in contest on one of the games and I can't let him think I've run away from the challenge. Can I?' His eyes danced with devilment and he struggled to control the teasing smile that tugged at his lips. He was obviously aware of the tension between his mother and Darrow and was delighting in it.

'Later, then. You did agree to dinner, didn't you?' Darrow smiled. The threat of confrontation was only noticeable to Megan, and she forced herself to nod in agreement while mentally she had already decided she would leave at once.

She watched him move with ease, carefully gliding from group to group with a naturalness that she envied. She had never recovered from her mother's criticism—even now it took all her will-power to combat her inner feelings of insecurity and present a confident façade. She was determined that her son would never feel the sense of worthlessness she had had to suffer. He was about to face up to adolescence—never an easy time—and to find out now that Darrow was his real father would have terrible repercussions.

The die was cast. The secret she had kept so long must remain deep within her heart. She had to protect her only son from anything that might make him feel rejected or unloved. Megan knew just how painful that could be.

Her mind drifted back to her unhappy childhood and the most memorable of the many arguments she had had with her mother.

'He doesn't care for you,' her mother had informed

her briskly as she sorted through a stack of papers, not even bothering to look at her distressed daughter. 'He just feels sorry for you. It's a pity, that's all,' she had continued, casting a brief look of disgust at her daughter's pale, sad face.

'He does care,' Megan had replied, her voice barely audible and lacking conviction.

'Don't be so pathetic,' she had scoffed, tossing the papers to one side and standing up in front of her daughter, ready for battle.

'I'm not—'

'Of course you are. It's no good looking at me like that; you know I'm right,' her mother had said confidently, charging on, careless of her daughter's feelings. 'I don't know why you're so dependent on him. Stand on your own two feet. I had to. I fought all the way on my own and so should you.'

'I'm not going to be on my own. Darrow will come back,' Megan had protested, her conviction fading against her mother's onslaught.

'Grow up, Megan. Out of sight, out of mind.' She had lifted Megan's hair between her fingers in despair. 'A little dowdy thing like you can hardly compete against those American beauties he'll be meeting.'

'He'll be back,' Megan had cried in utter frustration.

'Well, don't hold your breath. Your father never made an appearance, did he?' she had tossed at her as she marched away, and Megan had known, as usual, that she was a disappointment to her mother, that she could never be as strong as her. And surprisingly that still hurt.

CHAPTER THREE

MEGAN quickly finished her drink and began her search for Luke. She ignored all his protests, insisting that they should leave immediately. They had both reached the door before Darrow's voice resounded in the empty hall.

'I think it's a little too cold to eat al fresco,' his velvet voice taunted, and Megan swung round, uncharmed by the amused grin on his face. She exhaled slowly before glancing up and giving him a half-hearted smile. She ran her fingers through her hair, unconsciously curling its already natural wave. His grin widened still further as he recognised the familiar gesture of nervousness.

'We're tired. It's been a long day.' Her cheeks turned pink as she spoke, but her voice was firm despite the white lie.

'Who's this "we"?' objected Luke instantly, flashing her a look of discontent. 'I was on a roll, in Dracula's castle,' he complained, ignoring the grim expression on Megan's face as she glared at him.

'That's settled, then,' agreed Darrow, beaming a smile at Luke for his help in what Megan was convinced was a conspiracy against her. 'Try typing in PQRS, then go through the second door and...'

Megan was totally confounded by the code but knew it was something to do with the computer game. Her heart shrivelled a little inside her. She had tried numerous times to get to grips with the new game technology but had always failed miserably, and she knew it was an important part of Luke's life that she was unable to share.

She felt excluded. A cold sense of loss swept over her; she had never had to share Luke before and it hurt.

'And?' demanded Luke, unable to bear waiting.

'One hundred extra lives. And if you can't get to level five now you never will,' laughed Darrow, rubbing Luke's head in a natural gesture of affection, and Megan was stunned when instead of shying away Luke stretched up his neck, like a cat wanting further strokes.

'PQRS,' repeated Luke.

'You got it.' Darrow smiled as Luke ran off without so much as saying goodbye to Megan.

She tried to pretend she didn't care but she did, very much. The relationship between her and Luke was very intense—she had showered him with all her love from the moment he had been handed to her. That moment was branded on her mind.

'Well done, he's a lovely little boy,' the nurse had gushed as he'd placed the tiny bundle of life into her open, eager arms.

'My son,' Megan had whispered in his ear as she'd held him close to her breast. She had inhaled the warm, sweet smell of him, forgetting all her feelings of fatigue. She was now fully awake, alert to every little nuance of her son. 'Thank you,' she had breathed, clasping her child even tighter, mentally swearing that no one would ever come between them.

A shiver of apprehension ran the length of her spine when she thought of the consequences that could develop if Luke ever knew the truth. Darrow turned to face Megan, arching his arm so that she could link hers into his, but Megan was not taken in by the easy charm that had fooled her all those years ago. Her eyes flicked to his arm but she hesitated, still unsure of the strength of her resolve.

'Come on, Meggie,' he cajoled, his eyebrows arched in a challenging look which he knew she would be unable to resist.

'Lead the way.' She nodded bravely, knowing full well she was walking straight into the jaws of hell.

'Relax,' laughed Darrow, drawing out her chair and noting the strained expression on her face. 'It's not such an ordeal, is it?' he questioned lightly, but there was a definite undercurrent to his tone that Megan alone was sensitive to. She looked at him cautiously, her heart skipping a beat as she caught the stray scent of him.

'Yes, it is,' she confessed, then, noting the mocking rise of his eyebrows in horror, she hurriedly explained, 'No, no—it's not you,' she began, 'it's the whole thing...' Her voice faded away as her embarrassment grew still further. Her cheeks took on a rosy glow as he stared at her, willing her to continue, and enjoying her discomfort.

'The whole thing?' he prompted.

'Going out to dinner. It's like...'

'A dinner-date,' Darrow offered with a teasing lilt to his voice, and he picked up his white linen napkin and flicked it open. His action drew Megan's eyes and she looked at his long, slender fingers, perfectly manicured, and for a fleeting moment she longed to reach out and touch them, to have her hand locked in his as it would have been all those years ago, she thought painfully.

'A date.' She repeated the words softly, struggling to fight an inner desire to allow herself to remember their first date. She felt that nervous again, and wondered how he felt. 'It's been so long since I've had a date,' she admitted ruefully, with a half-hearted smile.

'I can't believe that.' He laughed sexily, leaning over

the table, and his warm breath caressed her cheek. Megan lowered her head, unable to face the interest that glowed in the depths of his eyes.

'It's hard bringing up a child alone. I rarely go out.'

'No male companions?' he asked curiously, inclining his head to study her response closely.

'A couple—friends—someone to tighten a screw or fix a faulty light,' she said, trying to inject a little humour into the serious turn the conversation was taking.

'Nothing serious?' he probed, unable to believe she had been so alone.

'I've never wanted a serious relationship; I prefer to be free.' She laughed, unaware of the frown that puckered his brow.

'And you're free now.' He reached out and placed his cool fingertips under her chin, pushing it firmly upwards till she was looking into his face. Megan pulled away. She didn't want to play games, not these adult games of flirtation, and she knew that was all they were.

'Don't, Darrow,' she chastised, using the tone of voice normally reserved for Luke after he had been in some trouble. She hadn't been sure he would obey her, so she was grateful that the waiter arrived, forcing Darrow to sit back and accept a menu.

'What do you recommend?' she asked, steering the conversation on to a suitable safe area and hoping he would be enough of a gentleman to respond. She was not disappointed.

'Everything—naturally,' he replied smoothly, behaving as if nothing had happened, while Megan's skin still burned with his touch and a deep, longing ache had been awakened in her body. 'The two chefs are excellent and all the produce is local and therefore very fresh,' he said with pride, his eyes scanning the menu with unconcealed interest.

'So you take an interest in the catering side as well?' Megan asked, briefly glancing up from the menu and immediately noticing how the flickering candlelight had softened all the sharp edges from his features, washing away the years, making him look so much more like the man she had once known. Her heart flipped over and she quickly returned her attention to the menu, suffocating the traitorous thoughts that were racing through her mind.

'I take an interest in every aspect of the business. You do when it's your own,' he explained.

'Yes, I suppose you do,' agreed Megan. She did in her own studio, which, after three years of extremely hard work, was finally paying dividends.

'Including all the sporting activities,' he reminded her, the warning light lambent in his dark eyes, and Megan had to admire the clever way he had manipulated the conversation back to their previous discussion. She was glad of the interruption caused by the return of the waiter, who stood waiting patiently, notebook at the ready.

'I'll have the mushrooms in garlic sauce and the stuffed chicken,' Megan told him, giving back her menu with a winning smile. The waiter returned her smile before turning to take Darrow's order. His expression was grim and the waiter's smile immediately vanished, to be replaced by a more sombre look.

'The same,' he snapped in a quiet, abrupt voice, flashing a look of disapproval at his over-friendly member of staff. 'And we'll have a bottle of the Californian Chardonnay,' he informed him crisply, acknowledging the waiter's sharp nod of the head with one of his own. His attention then reverted swiftly back to Megan, and she could see at once that he was tense.

'I want to enjoy our meal, so before it arrives I'd like
to discuss Luke. I'm not prepared to allow him to do all
the activities—I don't think he's up to it.'

Megan felt her stomach plummet, and she swallowed
the painful lump in her throat. She watched his glass as
he passed it under his nose, hating the superior look on
his face. She was furious at his high-handed attitude. He
had no claims on her son—he had forfeited that right so
very long ago, and that fact only heated Megan's temper
still further.

'For safety reasons, I suppose,' she sneered, distrusting
his motivation and wondering whether or not he resented
Luke. He caught the unspoken accusation in her tone and
responded immediately.

'Yes,' he snapped, his eyes bright with a sudden flare.
'You agree?' he demanded, his dark brows arching as he
sensed her lack of commitment.

'Yes,' bit back Megan, hating the smile of victory that
immediately sprang to his mouth, and he leant back in
his chair with an aura of self-confidence which she found
extremely irksome.

'Good. Now that's settled, let's enjoy ourselves.'

Megan looked away quickly, to prevent him from seeing the mutinous expression that was most certainly on
her face.

'A penny for them?' he asked quietly, but Megan knew
her secrets were worth far more than that, so she shook
her head and managed a smile.

'Nothing important,' she lied, before continuing,
'What about you? How come you have ended up owning
a complex?' She was genuinely interested. It was far removed from his ambitions of years ago. Their meal arrived and the interruption gave Megan the opportunity to
take a close look at Darrow's face. She could see the

reluctance flickering over his normally poker-faced expression and it fuelled her curiosity even more. Besides, she felt she had a certain right to know what had happened.

'I went to the States, found that despite the scholarship I had little money, so took a job as a camp counsellor,' he explained quickly.

'A camp counsellor?' laughed Megan.

'It's not as bad as it sounds. I worked every holiday and weekend at a camp. I took the kids mountaineering, fishing, sailing—you name it, I did it.' His voice lacked interest and Megan wondered why.

'So writing went by the board?' she asked, feeling a little bitter. She had thought it meant so much to him— more than her.

'No, not entirely, but I did get hooked on the great outdoors. America has some marvellous open spaces, so untouched. It's an incredible contrast to the busy cities,' he enthused.

'So your career took a change of direction?' She encouraged him to tell her more. She wanted to know what he had been doing in the years they had been apart.

'Not entirely, but I admit that the experience I gained made me see the potential in setting up a similar outdoor pursuit centre here, so, once I had earned enough money, that's what I did,' he told her, taking another mouthful of wine.

'How did you earn such a large amount?' she asked, intrigued.

He was silent.

'Well, Darrow?' she pushed gently as she began to eat.

'You know *Paradise Hills*—the soap?' he said, with a sheepish, almost embarrassed grin.

'Yes, I know it,' admitted Megan, puzzled. 'I heard it was quite good. A bit flash, but good escapism after a hard day. Not that I ever had the chance to watch it.'

'Why not?' he asked incredulously. 'It goes out five times a week, it was so popular.'

'Working,' laughed Megan. 'As always, evening classes were full. These mushrooms are delicious, by the way,' she added as she placed another one in her mouth and flicked her tongue over lips that were coated in garlic sauce.

'I wrote it. Well, I was one of the writers. There was a core group of about five of us,' he explained. Her approval had evaporated any self-consciousness and he was now prepared to talk quite freely.

'So how did that come about?' she asked, too preoccupied in spearing another mushroom to see the cloud of unhappiness that passed over his face.

'Accidentally,' he said grimly, irony in his tone. 'I worked on it for five years and by then I'd had enough. Enough of everything,' he said, suddenly sounding weary and defeated.

'Did something go wrong?' probed Megan, frowning as she looked at him, sensing some sort of inner pain and struggle that he was keeping close to him. 'Darrow?' she said, trying to shake him from the mood.

'I was just homesick. I'd made a sizeable amount of money, and sport was still playing an important part in my life, so—well, the rest is history,' he concluded, quickly taking a large gulp of his wine and grimacing as it hit the back of his throat.

Megan accepted his words, knowing he had his secrets, and she could understand him wanting to keep them. She too had secrets she was unwilling to share.

'It's a large corporation.'

'Well, as you know, the hotel has always been here, and the extension at the back takes care of the indoor pastimes—a snooker room, computers, videos that type of thing—I have to cater for all sorts.' He laughed.

'And the accommodation?'

'I took the idea of wooden cabins from the camps, though mine are of luxury standard—even the smallest,' he said with evident pride. 'It seems popular, especially with children. Lots of families come, as well as businessmen at the other end of the scale.'

'What for?'

'Companies often use outdoor pursuits places for management training courses,' he explained as Megan looked at him incredulously.

'I've never understood the connection between abseiling and the ability to motivate a workforce.' Megan grinned.

'You'd be surprised. Hidden traits are often revealed when under pressure—it sorts out the winners and the losers,' he informed her, matching her grin with one of his own.

'I bet they don't do their own catering,' Megan said.

'No, they relax in the bar, have a bar meal or come to the restaurant. Not everyone wants to self-cater so we offer people the choice.'

'So despite the recession you're still doing all right?' she asked, the envy in her voice a little apparent.

'I'm managing to ride it. The people that come here are hardly struggling. Outdoor pastimes are notoriously expensive, despite everything you might think,' he informed her.

'Walking costs nothing,' Megan said, thinking about the hours they had spent together walking the hills.

'No, but walking-boots do, and anyone who likes their

hobby spends money—hence the shop. Do you have one?' he asked as an afterthought.

'A shop? No, I hadn't given the matter any thought,' she said, suddenly mulling over the possibility.

'Footwear, leotards—all sorts of items. You should think about it,' he told her in a considered tone.

'So you've been here some time?' she asked, intrigued to know why her mother hadn't mentioned the fact that he had returned.

'Actually, no. I've had a manager in and I have only recently arrived—about two months ago,' he concluded. Megan nodded. So her mother wouldn't have known of his return. She was grateful for that. She wasn't sure her mother wouldn't have told Darrow the truth about Luke.

'And what about you, Meggie?' he asked, catching her unaware, and for a moment she was going to blurt out the whole truth.

'I left Rannaleigh within a few months of you,' she admitted. At least that part was true. She saw his mouth thin to a hard line.

'I know,' he ground out, the flare of anger sparked off by her admission.

Megan ignored his remark and continued, her voice almost a whisper. She began her well-rehearsed lines, repeated so often that she sometimes wondered herself about the story's validity. 'I met Karl and married him,' she confessed, wondering if it hurt him but refusing to look up to gauge for herself his reaction.

'It was all rather sudden,' he said coolly, his voice distinct and disapproving, and she tensed as she felt his hidden anger.

'Yes, we fell head over heels in love, married, and then Luke came along,' she finished up quickly, hating the lies but knowing she had no alternative. She hoped he wouldn't probe too deeply. She knew she could never keep up the pretence in the face of his anger and yet to tell him the truth would be so damaging to Luke that she could not take the risk. She had told him the same tale, and he had grown up believing his father had died shortly after his birth.

'Lucky you,' he commented drily, the sarcasm as thick as treacle in his tone, but Megan feigned ignorance and merely gave him a wonderfully warm smile and agreed whole-heartedly.

'Yes, wasn't I?' she crooned back, tilting her face upwards in challenge despite her inner fears.

'Still, after Karl's death—then what?' he said, and the smile faded from her face at his words.

'I started the health club. It's only small but it's a start,' she said briefly, not wishing to disclose too much.

'It can't have been easy,' he considered thoughtfully. 'But you succeeded,' he encouraged with a ready smile.

'It has been a hard slog, but well worth it,' she said, not dwelling too much on just how difficult it had been.

'I'm very proud of you. You've done very well,' he commented, the delight shining from his eyes.

Luke interrupted them, rushing over, grinning from ear to ear.

'I slayed everyone,' he said, helping himself to a bread roll, oblivious to the intimacy he had intruded upon. 'Anyway, I've come for the key. I thought I'd go back now, pick up a pizza and watch the football. You can take care of her, can't you?' he said, focusing his eyes on Darrow. Megan felt a flush of rose cover her cheeks, which grew even deeper as Darrow's hand fell across hers in a protective shield.

'I'll take excellent care of her, as always,' he reminded her gently, giving her hand a delicate squeeze.

The words sounded like a mockery to her, though, it was true, there had been times when she had hidden herself behind his protective shield, unable to face her tormentors any more.

For a moment Megan was back in the schoolyard, standing out in her plain clothes, her mother having refused to put her child in the school uniform. But the joy of individuality had been lost on Megan and her mother had been oblivious to her daughter's distress. The voices of the children had grown louder as more and more children joined in the cruel chant, till it had thundered through Megan's ears.

'Where's your daddy gone?'

'Where's your daddy gone?'

The words had stabbed at her heart and she'd pressed her hands against her ears in an attempt to shut out the incessant chorus of voices. She'd screwed up her eyes, closed them tightly to block out the malicious grins and the mocking smiles that had danced in front of her eyes.

The firm arm that had fallen protectively around her shoulders had made her open her eyes.

It was Darrow. Tall, strong, good-looking Darrow—captain of the football team and school hero, admired by the girls and the boys.

'Shut up. Shut up, all of you,' he had declared hotly as he drew Megan's trembling body even closer. His voice had held the ring of authority even then, and once she had been awarded his protection Megan had known she was safe.

If only she'd had a father most of her school-day misery would not have existed and she never would have become so dependent on Darrow—so in love with him, Megan mused. Yet all the school bullying had faded into insignificance with her unexpected pregnancy, and then where had he been?

Her protector, she thought bitterly, hating the moment that flashed so vividly through her mind, the gleam of triumph in her mother's eyes when she'd told her he would not be coming back, that he had found someone else.

Unbidden tears heated the back of her eyes but she refused to let them fall; it was too late now for tears. She drew her hand from under his and picked up her bag, producing the key while Luke and Darrow talked.

Her own thoughts were suddenly shattered by the rise in octave of Luke's voice. She looked up quickly, seeing the familiar red of his heated face when angry.

'I can,' he was insisting. 'I'm on the football and rugby team at school, I can swim over two miles—' No doubt he would have added to the list of his achievements had Darrow's cool voice not cut in.

'I'm sorry you're disappointed. You're obviously a good sportsman, but I cannot allow you to undertake so many new challenges.' Darrow's voice was soft but firm, but Megan knew Luke would just continue to badger him.

Luke turned to her, his eyes pleading. 'You tell him. Tell him how good I am. I *will* be able to cope, won't I?' His voice was growing stronger with indignation and Megan felt trapped. She was furious with Darrow. She had been going to tell Luke; she knew how to handle him, she lied to herself.

'Luke, you'll be able to try lots of new things...' she began, trying to explain in a conciliatory tone. Her voice faltered as he snatched the keys from her hand and glared at her with all the over-developed emotion that charged through adolescent bodies.

'Well, as long as you have a good holiday,' he snapped pointedly, before marching out.

Megan was on her feet in seconds, ready to go after him, but Darrow gripped her arm, preventing her from moving. She swung round to face him, her eyes blazing with anger.

'Let me go,' she said through clenched teeth, trying to pull away. 'I've got to go after him, to try and explain.'

'I've done that.'

'Done what?' snapped Megan, her eyes flying back to Luke as he disappeared from the restaurant.

'Explained.'

'Oh, yes, I know—and look at the trouble it's caused,' she threw back at him, her anger knowing no bounds as her heart was torn into shreds. He had ruined their holiday with his interfering. 'I'll have to go after him; he's upset,' Megan tried to reason, noticing that Darrow had not relinquished his grip. If anything, it seemed to be tightening.

'He'll get over it. Besides, he was downright rude to you just then, so let him stew for a while,' Darrow said, with a clarity that came from not being emotionally involved. 'Ah, dinner,' he said with a grin, indicating the chair with his head.

Megan sighed. It was wrong to waste the food, and yet she was concerned about Luke. His sudden flares of temper seemed to be becoming more and more frequent, and she seemed to be losing control over him.

'Does he often fly off the handle?' enquired Darrow, slicing through his perfect white chicken to reveal the pink salmon which had been carefully stuffed inside.

'Unfortunately,' admitted Megan, glad of someone to confide in.

'I shouldn't worry. I was the same at his age. It's part

of growing up. There again, I was lucky—I always had my father to keep me in check,' he told her, and Megan remembered with affection the warm family home he had come from. It had been her shelter in the stormy life she had lived.

'Well, Luke isn't that lucky,' snapped Megan, hating being reminded of the fact and realising that Luke was coming to an age when a father was going to be missed.

'You're having a few problems with him?' Darrow asked, concern etched on his face as he studied her intently.

'I wish it were only a few,' Megan said wistfully, thinking of the numerous rows they had had recently.

'Adolescence is a difficult time,' mused Darrow.

'It certainly is for me,' Megan replied, trying to make light of her difficulties as usual.

'It's not easy to grow into yourself, seeking the approval of your peers while retaining your individuality and the love of your parents,' he told her.

'He no longer wants or needs my love or approval,' confessed Megan sadly, her teeth sinking into her lip.

'Of course he does, but he wants to show you he's growing up, that's all.'

'I know that but...'

'It's hard letting go?' he offered.

'He isn't tied to my apron-strings, if that's what you think,' she retorted hotly, remembering his criticisms from before.

'Certainly not. But you are obviously very close— bound to be when there's just the two of you.' His understanding of the situation amazed her.

'I suppose that's why it's so hard. We've always been so close—real friends,' Megan told him.

'You still are. He just needs a little more space, that's

all,' Darrow told her, treating her to a gentle smile that
softened her resolve against him.

'I suppose,' she admitted thoughtfully, hoping she
could ride the storm with Luke. 'Like me, perhaps he
wants a father,' she said without thinking, and Darrow
smiled.

'Meggie, surely you're not still bothered about that?'
he said softly, the warmth in his voice threatening to
overwhelm her. 'It's not even considered important any
more,' he said persuasively.

'It was to me. But you wouldn't understand—it wasn't
you the other children called ''bastard'', was it?' Her
voice nearly broke as she spoke the terrible word that
had haunted her childhood.

'It might as well have been. I felt your pain, Meggie,
you know that.' His voice was as soft as the moonlight
that was spilling across their table, his words bringing
back a memory she knew to be true. She felt weakened,
overcome with the tidal wave of emotions that had been
building up all day since her arrival. 'We were always
kindred spirits,' he added softly, leaning closer, his breath
warming her cheek, his hand gently tracing over the side
of her face in a warm caress.

'Darrow,' whispered Megan, closing her eyes to shut
out the present and allow herself the dream of the past.
It was easy to drift back, to allow herself a moment of
weakness. His aftershave filled her lungs as she breathed
deeply, enjoying the familiar scent. Without thinking,
Megan lowered her face, kissing his hand as it swept
down her chin, loving the rough touch of his hair and the
salty taste of his skin.

She knew it was madness, but she was powerless to
do anything but respond to him. Her whole being ached,
had never ceased aching for him since he had left, and

now at last she had him back again. He moved his hand and Megan's eyes immediately sprang open. She hated the sudden chill that swept through her body and stared at him, suddenly confused.

She concentrated on her food, denied herself a dessert, tempting though they were, and sipped her coffee. Conversation had been easy—too easy—and she knew she was in danger of behaving foolishly, but somehow she seemed unable to stop herself.

'Come on, Meggie,' he invited softly. 'Let's go somewhere a little more private.' He extended his hand as he slowly rose from his chair with a liquid grace. She hesitated, but the pull of physical attraction was much too strong and she smiled and lifted her hand to his. His strong fingers wrapped around hers, instantly warming her blood with their familiarity. He tugged at her and she moved towards him.

Together they left the restaurant, walking in unison, their bodies in perfect step. It was so natural, just how it should be, and, dangerous though it would be, Megan decided to allow herself this one last brief moment of love. She would have a holiday romance. For two heady, glorious weeks she would let time stand still and just enjoy his company. It was like a dream come true and she would enjoy it while it lasted.

She knew Luke would be a problem but this was her last chance. She could never again come back to Rannaleigh, not now that Darrow was here, and within a couple of years she would be unable to deny him Luke— the family resemblance would be too great. For a moment she faltered and he sensed her reluctance; he turned to her, smiling softly.

'Let's go for a walk,' he suggested, and she nodded silently in reply, unable to break the magic of the moment with needless words. The cold night air caused Megan to shiver; her fine silk dress afforded no protection from the chill wind.

'Here,' Darrow said generously, pulling his jacket from his body and wrapping it around her. Megan opened her mouth to protest but he pressed his strong fingers against her soft lips to silence her. She could smell the very essence of him on his jacket, feel the heat of his body in the warm silk, and they acted like an aphrodisiac, stirring feelings deep with her body.

They walked in silence. The moon was rising from between grey clouds and illuminating the lake with its silvery rays. She knew where they were going—their secret place…a tiny slope that afforded them complete privacy as well as an unsurpassable view of the lake.

'A bench!' cried Megan in surprise. That was a new addition, and for a moment it hurt her, the thought of other people here, but he quickly allayed her fears.

'No one knows it's here—this place is too well-hidden. I often come here,' he admitted ruefully, and Megan grinned as she sat down, recalling all the times she had hidden here, safe from the taunts of others that she had been forced to suffer because of her mother's unconventional views.

Yet, despite everything, she missed her—missed her outrageous remarks, her bizarre behaviour. She wondered what her mother would have made of her now, sitting here with Darrow, contemplating embarking on a two-week affair, and she knew with a sure certainty that this was one of the few occasions when she would have had her mother's approval.

She felt the firmness of Darrow's hand on her back and stiffened at the unbearably casual touch. His breath caressed the hollow of her neck as he moved closer and for a moment Megan closed her eyes, trying to shut out the erotic images of them together which raced through her mind. Her spine tingled with anticipation as his fingers slowly stroked down her back and he drew her closer, her body moulding into his with ease. His arm was round her waist now, making her stomach flip. She felt like a young girl again, a little fearful and yet wonderfully excited. She turned, knowing that his face was drawing closer, knowing they were going to kiss.

The pull of physical attraction was so sharp that in that moment the years fell away; time was suspended. It was as if nothing mattered, only them. A host of warm feelings welled up inside her as she caught the deep, slumberous invitation in his eyes. Her whole being was alive, tingling with joyful expectation. She began to tremble as her defences began to weaken and disintegrate. Instinctively her arms reached out for him. She longed to hold him, to grasp him, to feel the muscular strength of his chest against her.

Their lips touched and her breath stopped briefly. She was afraid to move. The pressure of his mouth increased as he drew her closer and she moved against him, her body fitting neatly into his. Her arms wrapped around him, clinging to him as if she would never let him go. This moment was far too precious to waste. It was different, this kiss, even more potent than she remembered, more skilful, more mature and her own responses were those of a woman, not a young girl. She was able to give as well as receive now, and it added to their mutual fulfilment.

The heat between them intensified, their bodies forcing themselves against each other, their kisses deepening with passion. Megan was becoming lost in a sea of unaccountable emotion. She wanted him, needed him more

than she had ever needed him before. He was chasing
away all her pain, all her doubts with his customary ease
and Megan was aware of her dependence upon him
resurfacing with every passing moment. She was quite
unprepared for the feeling of loss that swept over her as
he pulled away, though she sensed his reluctance.

'Like a fine wine,' he murmured, their heads still so
close that his warm breath touched her skin.

'Wine?' managed Megan in a hoarse whisper, still
breathless, her fingers entwined around his neck, not
wanting to let go.

'You've improved with age,' he grinned, tracing her
lips with his fingers. 'Yet you taste as fresh as ever,' he
sighed. 'Totally untouched,' he added wistfully, and Megan knew he was thinking about Karl and moving on to
dangerous ground. She gave an almost silent laugh as a
tremor rippled through her body.

'You're just trying to hang on to your youth,' she
teased. 'That's all.'

Darrow's dark eyes narrowed on hers as he studied her
intently, distrusting her sudden flippancy after what they
had just shared.

'Are you sure that's all?' he questioned coolly, waiting
for her response, and Megan felt a sudden tension. She
nodded as she dropped her arms. The magic was now
gone for her, leaving only a feeling of dread.

'Of course. Good food, a few glasses of wine and a
chance to meet up with your first love, recapturing your
lost youth.'

'I'm not sure I believe that, and I know you don't,' he
warned her gently, and a frisson of alarm raced the length
of her body. He was dangerously close, and she couldn't
help but wonder if she had overestimated herself. Maybe
she couldn't afford to take the risk of having a holiday

romance with Darrow; her feelings were already too deep for such a carefree romance.

'I'll see you home,' he told her, aware that something had changed but failing to understand what.

'Yes, I think that would be for the best,' she agreed, suddenly wanting to be alone, to try and fathom how she felt about him, and how prepared she was to jeopardise her relationship with her son—a relationship that was already on thin ice, she was forced to admit.

The walk back was conducted in silence. No words seemed suitable and banal conversation seemed anathema. The solitary cry of a hunting owl was the only sound that shattered the night.

'Thanks for this evening, Meggie. I enjoyed myself,' he said as they arrived at her lodge, and he placed his hands possessively on her hips, drawing him closer to her. She turned her head, looking fearfully up at the lodge, hoping that Luke was not watching them.

'I enjoyed myself too,' she admitted, not wanting to say too much and reveal her weakness for him.

'Good, because I see no reason why we shouldn't do it again some time,' he murmured as he took her in his arms and planted a sudden soft kiss on her lips. She lifted her head to meet his, revealing the slender curve of her neck. She opened her mouth, flicking her tongue across her full lips in a provocative invitation which he immediately responded to.

It was a gentle kiss, filled with promises for a future of full commitment and fulfilment.

He drew back with a smile that warmed her body. 'Goodnight, Meggie; sleep well,' he called as the darkness of the night swallowed him up.

Megan turned, pulling his jacket around her body and revelling in the very scent of him. She was in a quandary.

What on earth was she doing? she chastised herself. This time—this time it would be different, she concluded. This time she would remain in control. She would get Darrow Maine out of her system once and for all.

But even as the words echoed through her mind a niggling doubt was beginning to develop. She suddenly felt vulnerable, and it frightened her.

CHAPTER FOUR

THE morning air was fresh and crisp, and despite the promise of sunshine later there was quite a cold nip in the early morning air. Megan had left Luke at the sports centre, waiting with the others for a morning river-rafting trip. He had been so excited, she could tell, despite the over-relaxed manner which he had felt he must portray. Megan had smiled secretly at his behaviour but had made no comment on it, leaving him quickly so he would not be embarrassed by her presence. He was far too old to have his mother with him.

There was no point in taking the car, Megan thought. Her mother's house was far from the beaten track, situated deep in a wooded glen, and the only access was by a rough, rambling path. It was not a visit Megan was looking forward to. It had been so many years since she had been home and she knew it would be painful to see the little house again.

She also knew that it would be hard work clearing the house. Her mother had been a born hoarder, and Megan knew it would probably take days to clear everything, but at least while she was at her mother's there would be no chance of meeting Darrow, and it would give Luke much needed breathing-space. Yet, despite these plus features, Megan was still dreading it.

'You're up early.' Darrow's clear voice cut through the still, quiet morning, shattering Megan's private thoughts. She met his eyes straight on, hiding the inner turmoil that she felt at his sudden, unexpected presence.

He looked good—too good, she mused, aware of the impact he made. He was wearing a thick, heavy knitted jumper and the white collar of a polo shirt pulled out around his neck emphasised his weathered outdoor tan. A thick waterproof jacket with reinforced zips in a contrasting shade matched his well-worn jeans that were tucked neatly into a pair of strong boots. His black hair was still damp from the shower and he had combed it back, revealing the chiselled features of his face. Megan noticed a scar, a fine white line, that ran across his forehead and then jaggedly down towards his right eye.

'Yes, bright and early.' She half smiled, her eyes still on the scar, wondering where it had come from. 'So are you,' she added, pulling her eyes away from the mark which instead of detracting from his looks, only seemed to add to his attractiveness.

'A souvenir from America,' he said coldly as he ran his long fingers over the mark with a well-practised hand. Megan nodded, embarrassed that he had been aware of her staring. She watched his fingers in quiet fascination. Their slow movements made her recall last night's events, and she suddenly realised that she wasn't sure how to handle their relationship now.

'Along with the clothes, I presume?' Megan said, nimbly altering the conversation to something less personal. She wasn't ready to drift down that path again. The tug of attraction was still there, she could feel it, see it in his eyes too, but whether it went beyond the purely physical she did not know. She had never known any man but him. Any other relationship she had always been at pains to keep on the 'good friends' level. Not that it had been particularly difficult, Megan mused. She had been far too busy building up her health club business and raising a son to have much time for any other commitments.

'That's right. Their outdoor wear is really effective against the elements, and I'll need all the protection I can get this morning.' He grinned, the warmth of his smile heating her blood, and in that brief moment the years seemed to fall away as her own mouth curled in a neutral response.

'What's on your agenda?'

'I'm off river-rafting.' His smile deepened. 'A party of ten,' he added, with the usual attractive arrogance of a man who was in total control and knew it.

'It includes Luke,' she reminded him tightly, wondering whether or not he would approve of him going. The edge in her voice, though, was because of her own fears. She tried to remain calm but was unable to prevent herself from reacting. Her response did not go unnoticed, and a tell-tale light flared briefly in Darrow's cool blue eyes.

'Does it?' he asked, his eyebrows lifting slightly in surprise, but Megan was not fooled by his pretence. She knew he would have a full list of all participants, and probably a rough idea of how much each one was capable of.

'Is that a problem?' she asked. She looked relaxed, as if making a polite enquiry, but there was a guarded look in her eyes, a sharpness entering the tone of her voice, and the smile now began to fade from her face.

'No,' he answered shortly, holding her eyes as he looked directly at her. 'Should it be?' He raised an eyebrow slightly in challenge, as if amused by her overprotectiveness.

Megan was numb, unable to think of a suitable response. There was indeed a problem. She hadn't thought that Darrow would be taking such an active part in the

activities, and she wondered how long it would be before
he or someone else saw the resemblance.

She felt a glow of heat colour her normally pale complexion. She felt he was stripping her bare, revealing the
secret that she knew she had to keep.

'What is it, Megan? What are you frightened of?' His
voice was sharp, yet there was an underlying anxiety
there. 'I'll look after him,' he continued.

Megan searched his face. There was something that
triggered alarm in her. Definitely something in his tone
which only she would recognise because she knew him
so well—a thread of apprehension. But his face showed
complete composure and his eyes were still, deep pools.
There was an embarrassed angry silence, a void that neither of them could fill.

'Yes, of course,' she agreed, forcing a lightness into
her voice as past memories threatened to flood her mind.
'I just want to make sure he has a good holiday,' she
added by way of explanation, and to relieve the tension
she was feeling. She tucked the wisps of hair that curled
on her cheeks, framing her face, back behind her ears in
a nervous gesture.

'He will,' he agreed, easily enough, a smile touching
the corners of his mouth. 'I'll make sure of it.'

'Thank you.' She tried to relax, to force a smile on her
face, but instead of reassuring her his words only gave
rise to new doubts and fears. 'I'd best be going,' she said.
She wanted to escape from his presence, which seemed
to be pulling her nerve-endings tighter and tighter.

'Where are you off to?' he asked casually, totally unaware of the agitation he was arousing in her.

'My mother's,' Megan answered quickly, forcing
down the torrent of emotions that raged within her as she
thought of her mother and the way she had been so cru-

elly robbed of any last farewells. That was the real tragedy of sudden death—not having the opportunity to say
goodbye. It was probably how her mother had wanted
it—she had never been able to bear any form of what she
considered sentimentality, so maybe it was for the best.
Megan comforted herself with the thought, unaware that
Darrow was looking at her intently, reading her private
thoughts with uncanny accuracy.

'Alone?'

'Alone.' She repeated the single word, which held a
poignancy she had not expected. 'Who else would want
to come?' she tried to joke, but her voice began to crack.

'That won't be easy.' His eyes glinted with admiration
spiked with pity, and Megan fought back. The last thing
she wanted was his pity.

'No,' she admitted, her voice strong, fuelled by his
unwanted sympathy. 'But it has to be done,' she told him.
Then her lips curled as she added with a wry smile, 'So
much cleaning.'

'She was never one for domestic chores,' he remembered with affection, the low hum of laughter in his
voice. Megan looked up at him, watching the play of
emotions flicker like shadows across his face as he recalled the past they had shared.

'No,' she agreed, a smile broadening her face, showing
her two tiny dimples to perfection as they were cradled
in her soft cheeks. 'Life was far too exciting to waste on
such trivial pursuits as housework.' She laughed, and an
unexpected stab of envy of her mother's carefree attitude,
one that she had never managed to achieve, suddenly
pierced her.

'She always had you,' he reminded her, and then she
understood the source of her jealousy. She had played
the role of mother to perfection—taking charge of the

home, trying to keep it clean and tidy, despite the laid-back attitude of her mother.

'I enjoyed it,' Megan said, feeling guilty and wanting to protect her mother's memory. 'I like things neat and tidy.' Megan allowed herself a secret smile at those words when she thought of the turmoil that raged in her private life.

'You were so different.'

'Not as different as you think,' she corrected him, glancing at him sideways and meeting his half-smile.

If only he knew how tragically she had followed in her mother's footsteps, giving birth to a fatherless child. The only difference was that she did not share her mother's pride in the event, did not feel the same justification in robbing her son of his father. And yet he had forced her into that terrible situation, she thought bitterly. Whereas her mother had delighted in her single state, Megan saw it as a source of embarrassment that she would not inflict on her child.

'I really must be off,' she told him, wanting to be alone, to give herself time to think. The conversation was becoming too personal, too chancy, and Megan could sense the hidden potential danger there.

'Are you going to be there all day?' he asked as she moved away, as if he wanted to prolong the conversation, and she halted, turning to look at him, partly glad of the delay.

'At least till lunchtime,' she told him. 'I have to be back for Luke.'

'I see.' He nodded before asking, 'What are you planning on doing with the house?' He caught her hesitation, and saw her white teeth nibbling at the corner of her mouth. It was an expression of her fraught emotions that he remembered well from the old days.

'I don't know,' she answered honestly. She had decided it was to be sold, but now she wasn't so sure. For some reason she now had doubts.

'You're not going to come back and settle here, then?'

Megan raised her head swiftly, searching his face for some emotion to read, but there was nothing. He was as expert as her at hiding his feelings behind a façade of polite enquiry.

'No—no, I don't think so.' She was careful to keep her tone casual. It would do no one any good to allow her feelings full rein. Besides, they were so confused she had no real idea how she felt.

'You could keep it as a holiday home,' Darrow suggested, eyeing her curiously.

She turned her head, shaking it almost sadly as she realised that it made little difference to him. She knew she couldn't. The idea was ridiculous. The thought of coming here, where Darrow was—how long could that go on before he recognised himself in Luke? She could see the resemblance already...

'I could, I suppose—' she began, but her voice lacked commitment and he sensed it, cutting in smoothly, his gentle burr now edged with an American drawl,

'Think about it. It's a little off the beaten track for most. I doubt whether a local would want to buy it, and I hate the thought of the whole area becoming a community of strangers,' he finished softly. His views were not unknown to her—it was happening in all the rural areas. House prices were soaring beyond the means of the locals as rich city people bought second homes.

'Yes, I understand,' she agreed compassionately. 'But as the nearest shop is two miles away I can only imagine tourists being interested. In the winter months it's awful,' she remembered with a shiver.

'It wasn't all bad.' He smiled, a teasing grin, slow and sexy. 'It meant I had to stop over many a night.' His grin widened still further, smoothing away all the hard angles on his angular features till he looked more as she remembered him, and the memory of those cold winter nights became vividly alive.

She recalled the solid strength of him as his arms had wrapped round her, shutting out the cold as she was held secure in his love. She stepped back, aware that the thought could so easily become a reality. She had read his intentions in the slow way he had stepped slightly closer to her.

'That's true,' she agreed, trying to remain aloof, as if it was all in the past and she was unperturbed by him mentioning their past history. She breathed in deeply, letting the cold mountain air freeze the heady emotions he was raising in her. 'I think I probably will sell. Someone must want it.'

'Perhaps,' he agreed, 'but surely there's no rush?'

'I do have commitments. I'm struggling with repayments, and the recession has hit the membership.'

'I understand, but surely the house means something to you?' he said, hating the thought of the final link between them being destroyed.

'Yes, it means the chance of me having some money so I don't have to worry,' she returned, unable to stop herself.

'Megan, there was a time when this place meant everything to you,' he protested. 'To us,' he added.

'Did it? You left for America first,' she reminded him spitefully.

'I was coming back—we talked about it often enough. We were always together, sharing dreams for the future,' he reminded her.

'That's right,' she snapped back. 'Dreams. Good job we both woke up.'

'Yes, it is,' agreed Darrow, glaring at her, but Megan was too angry to notice.

'Here's your party.' She looked at the crowd of young people who were making their way towards them, her eyes seeking out and finding Luke instantly. She took her leave, glancing back only the once to see Darrow surrounded by the noisy group, head and shoulders taller than everyone else and in total command. She increased her pace. She had wasted enough time already. She stepped out briskly, the sense of relief adding to her enjoyment, but it was short-lived.

The first sight of the house nestled among the trees made her heart contract painfully. The small outhouse that her mother had used as a studio seemed strangely silent, and the house looked forlorn, unloved. Megan swallowed the painful emotions that surged through her body as she forced the key into the lock and pushed the door open; the pile of post hampering her entrance added to the empty atmosphere. The familiar scent of home still hung in the air; everything was as she remembered— which only added to her distress. It was so quiet, so strange, and yet at any moment she expected to hear her mother's footfall or hear her call her name.

Megan began clearing in earnest. Keeping herself busy would suffocate the well of sorrow that threatened to engulf her. Each book, each little ornament, each picture, every single item seemed suddenly touched with a specialness, a sadness that was so hard to cope with.

Megan picked up an old photograph. Its colour was faded a little—the deep blues to pale, the whites a yellowy grey—but the moment was etched on her mind forever. It was the moment she had said goodbye to Darrow.

They were standing side by side, his arm wrapped affectionately around her slim shoulders, and she had her arm about his waist. They both looked so young, so innocent. Tears stung sharply at the back of her eyes but Megan refused to let them fall, blinking them away quickly, afraid to give vent to her feelings.

She rummaged further down into a box—old bills, forgotten diaries, postcards from distant relatives. Nothing of any real importance. But then, pushed deep down into the very corner of the box, there was an old envelope, brown with age but still clearly addressed to Megan. She stared at the envelope, puzzled by it, and immediately tore it open. She sank back on to her knees as she read the contents. Her heart was thudding in her ears and she felt dizzy.

She had a father, a real father, a man who had actually wanted to know her. She scanned the date on the letter. It was quite old, but she was determined to telephone the solicitor mentioned—he still might know something, and Megan was determined to find her father if she could.

A rap on the door made her jump, and she quickly stowed the picture and her feelings away before going to answer it.

'Hello there, Megan. It's good to see you.' A familiar friendly face beamed at her and she gave a gasp of surprised delight.

'Janet! How on earth did you know I was here?' she said, giving her a hug then stepping back to let her enter. The familiar sense of shame dwelt briefly in her mind as she remembered how house-proud Darrow's mother had been, compared to her own.

'Darrow let me know—thought you shouldn't be here on your own,' she told her in her usual efficient tone. 'He's right, of course. This type of job requires company or it becomes maudlin.' She made her way through to the tiny lounge, her eyes quickly taking full stock of the work that needed doing and already mentally making notes about what to do.

Megan watched her expert eyes scanning round, delighted that she was here. The job would be done in half the time now.

The two women worked hard, and before long a whole stack of unwanted items was piled in one corner.

'It's really kind of you to come and offer help. Would you like a coffee? Tea?' Megan asked. 'It's dried milk, I'm afraid,' she added a little self-consciously.

'Nonsense. You don't think I came empty-handed, do you?' Janet said with a mock-frown as she passed over a basket with a broad smile that lifted her plump, rosy cheeks. 'And I'll have a large piece of that fruit cake,' she called after Megan, who had gone to put on the kettle. 'No point in watching my figure at my age—no one else does.' She chuckled as she turned back to the pile of papers in front of her.

The tiny kitchen was at least clean, mused Megan as she emptied Janet's basket. She had filled it with basics—tea, coffee, milk, sugar, some biscuits and a home-made Dundee cake. The contrast between her own mother and Darrow's had always been extreme. Janet was a real home-maker—a place for everything, and everything in its place—while Megan's mother had lived in a happy jumble, never knowing or caring where anything was. There had always been a sunset to capture, or a flower in bloom. She would paint for hours, forgetting to prepare meals or wash dishes. All that responsibility had fallen to Megan, and yet despite their different personalities they had finally grown to love each other. It was only now that Megan was beginning to understand just how much, and to appreciate her mother as an individual.

'Darrow is trying to make this place somewhere special,' Janet told her with evident pride as they both sat down to enjoy their tea and cake. Megan gave her a brief smile, her lack of response more telling than she realised. 'You didn't know he was here, did you?' Janet persisted, fixing her with wise, clear eyes that demanded an honest answer.

'No, I didn't know he had come back from the States,' she admitted, keeping her voice deliberately light and uncaring. But the interest that flitted across Janet's face warned her that she was not so easily fooled.

'He did well over there—a few scripts. I wish he'd done more, but most of his energy was taken up with Carrie—' She stopped abruptly, as if embarrassed by that admission. She looked so uncomfortable that Megan felt compelled to rescue her.

'It's all right, Janet. It was a long time ago.' The ready lie sprang quickly to Megan's lips as she toyed with a loose raisin on her plate, avoiding the pull of Janet's intelligent eyes with difficulty. Though the knowledge that he had even neglected his writing for Carrie caused her pain.

Megan jumped in alarm, her eyes flying to the door, then back to the amused look on Janet's face, as she heard Luke's voice calling. She guessed that Darrow had given him directions to the place; it was not that hard to find, even though it was some distance from the road.

'Mum! Mum!' he called, slamming the door in his wake. And gone was any hope that Megan had had of keeping her secret. Darrow's mother would be bound to recognise her own grandson.

Megan shot to her feet, struggling with the fear that

she was about to be found out. Luke smiled as he came in, his hair wet and stuck to his face—which only seemed to emphasise the resemblance to his father. Megan covertly flashed a look at Janet. She was studying him with a deep interest that Megan found unnerving.

'It was fantastic. First we all rowed till we hit the white water—that's what the rapids are called,' he told them importantly, before racing on. 'Then we had to use our oars for steering. Afterwards we all had a swim, but Darrow insisted no one dived in 'cos there may have been hidden rocks below,' he explained, unable to keep the admiration from his voice.

'Excuse my son's bad manners,' Megan put in, putting too much emphasis on the words 'my son', but unable to prevent herself as she felt threatened. 'Luke, this is Mrs Maine—Darow's mother,' she said, hating the deep look that Janet was giving him.

'I presume this was your first time river-rafting?' she asked, her polite enquiry holding a sting, Megan felt. Luke nodded enthusiastically. 'I thought so. Darrow reacted in much the same way.' She smiled briefly at Luke, but her gaze swiftly found Megan's eyes as she spoke, leaving the words hung in the air. 'Well, I'd best be off. Let me know when you're coming again. I'll gladly help you,' she told Megan as she put her coat back on.

'Thank you. I'll give you a ring,' Megan lied as she escorted her to the door, wanting her away from Luke. The least she saw of him the better. Janet paused before she made her way down the path and Megan felt her heartbeat increase tenfold as she waited for Janet to speak.

'You must come round for a bite to eat—lunch, perhaps. You and Luke would be most welcome,' she said, with a ready smile that Megan instinctively responded to even though she knew that it was impossible. She nodded but made no firm arrangements. The whole idea was preposterous.

'Yes, that will be lovely,' she called as she closed the door, leaning back heavily on it and exhaling noisily, her breath lifting the hair from her face.

'What's up?' asked Luke, watching her actions with a quizzical look.

'Read this,' Megan instructed, passing him the letter with a trembling hand.

'Gosh, what a surprise. Are you going to get in touch?' he asked with a wide grin.

'Do you think I should?' asked Megan, longing for some support. The thought of meeting her father was quite intimidating.

'Of course you should. I want to meet my grandad— he might be extremely wealthy,' commented Luke hopefully.

'He might not.'

'I'd take the chance. I'd still like to meet him,' admitted Luke thoughtfully.

'Me first, I think…'

'I understand,' said Luke with a sudden flash of maturity.

'Thanks,' smiled Megan, her heart pounding at the thought of having a father.

'It's neat here,' he continued.

'Is it?' she asked, pushing herself from the door and going back to retrieve her flying jacket. She slipped her arms into the sleeves as she spoke. 'I had you down as a real city boy.' She laughed, zipping up her jacket and picking up her keys.

'I am. But at heart I'm a real country lad,' said Luke, placing his hand on his heart in a mocking gesture.

'Really?' laughed Megan, enjoying his action as she pulled open the door, giving the house one final look-round. She knew it wouldn't be as hard next time she came—something about the place was still home. 'Come on, let's get some lunch.'

'I'm starved,' Luke agreed.

'Aren't you always?' said Megan. Her son's appetite never seemed to be satiated.

'I like Granny's house—it really sums her up. Doesn't it?' he said as he glanced back over his shoulder. Megan caught the sorrow in his voice and wrapped an affectionate arm around his shoulders.

'Yes, it does,' she agreed. 'It was my home.' And for the first time in her life she said those words with real pride. She gave a smile of sudden appreciation for her unorthodox upbringing.

Megan prepared a quick lunch, marvelling at how well-equipped the lodge kitchen was, and how well-designed.

'Are you coming down to the lake?' Luke asked as he helped himself to an apple and sank his teeth into the bright red skin with obvious delight.

'Yes, I might as well. I'll bring a book, though,' Megan informed him. She didn't want him thinking she would be there just to watch him, but she knew it would be difficult not to. 'Aren't you going to have a rest first? Just a sit down?' she added hurriedly, seeing the look of horror on his face.

'No time,' he answered briefly, already picking up his sports bag and making for the door. Megan held her tongue and picked up her book, shoving it deep into her shoulder-bag as she followed him.

The sun was high in the afternoon sky and the weather was hot, but a gentle breeze from the lake was refreshingly cool. Megan settled herself on a grassy mound, with the marine centre clearly in view so that she could keep a close eye on her son. The last thing she wanted was any relapse.

'Luke—Luke, your hands are too close,' roared a familiar voice, and Megan's head spun round. She saw Darrow standing on the edge of the lake, watching the canoeing class with his eagle-sharp eyes. She scanned the water. The brightly coloured canoes were all bumping against each other; no one was showing any particular skill, she thought indignantly as she watched her own son's attempts with pride.

'Is this right?' she heard Luke yell back, his hands raised up high above his head to show Darrow his position.

'No,' came back the abrupt reply. 'They're still too close.'

Megan watched, her heart in her mouth, as Luke struggled with the large oar, moving his hands while his canoe seemed to rock unsteadily in the water.

'There. Stop…that's right.'

Megan couldn't catch the following conversation which passed between them, but she was sure that Darrow was finding fault with Luke. She sensed that he disliked him—he had made that obvious from the start, refusing to allow him to take part in all the pastimes available. She marched over, her ears straining to catch any snatches of conversation but unable to.

'Look where you're going, Luke. Hold your concentration,' barked Darrow, pointing angrily at Luke as he careered into another canoe. Even from the shore Megan could see Luke's skin turn pink, and her heart went out to him.

'Pull back round the other way. Watch the oar!' yelled

Darrow as Luke seemed to go out of control, making Megan's heartbeat race. She stood at the side of Darrow, tight-lipped, her face icing over with an hauteur that surprised him. He threw her a quick glance, unperturbed by her presence, his attention already back on the canoes.

'Right, now just paddle. Spread out, but no further than the flag.' He called his instruction and the canoes began to separate, each finding its own area. Then Darrow turned to face her.

'How did you get on at your mother's?' he asked, his question catching her off guard as she had expected him to mention Luke. So she responded immediately, forgetting for a moment just how angry she was with him.

'All right. Your mother came across,' she told him, her eyes drifting back to the lake and the bobbing canoes.

'Hmm,' he answered, preoccupied, as he turned his full attention back on to the group in the water.

'Luke!' he suddenly roared, making Megan jump. 'Stay within the flagged area.'

Luke responded to the order with a short wave of his hand, but Megan was furious. She was convinced that Darrow didn't like Luke because of what had happened between themselves all those years ago.

'He is,' she declared hotly.

'What?' queried Darrow, his attention firmly fixed on the canoes and only half listening to Megan. 'Lift that side, Jamie…that's better. What were you saying?' he asked Megan distractedly, still not giving her any real attention.

'Luke *was* in the flagged area,' she protested, her lips pressed tightly closed together in a thin line.

'I know.'

'You said—'

'I told him to stay in the flagged area,' he cut in

sharply, noticing her anger for the first time. 'As a reminder, that's all.'

'Safety?' mocked Megan, her anger inflamed by his
arrogance.

'That's right.' He flashed her a grin, then turned his
attention back to the lake, unperturbed by her outburst.

Megan did not respond. She knew what the real problem was—the fact that to him Luke was a solid reminder
of her love for someone else. How part of her yearned
to tell him the truth, but she could not afford to jeopardise
the fragile relationship she had with her son.

'You don't like Luke, do you?' she accused him, a
freezing pain gripping her chest as she thought of the
distrust between father and son and wondered who was
the most responsible.

Darrow spun round, a flicker of confusion flaring in
his eyes before being replaced by a frosty anger. His
expression was stunned, but Megan knew she had come
too close to a home truth that Darrow was unable to
admit, even to himself.

'What makes you say that?' Cold anger hardened his
expression as he spoke, his tone savage and raw as Megan's observation hit a nerve.

'Isn't it obvious? You never give him a chance,' she
declared, arching a haughty brow at him but forcing herself to remain calm.

'Don't be ridiculous, Megan,' he stormed. 'I'm just
doing my job. Luke seems a little...'

'What?' she cried indignantly, incensed that he now
considered he knew Luke better than her. She frowned
at him darkly, waiting for him to speak, almost daring
him to find fault with her son as it would justify what
she had just accused him of.

'If you must know, he seems determined to prove himself—to who I don't know.' He shrugged, but Megan already had a gnawing idea that Luke might want to impress Darrow. 'Maybe himself,' he added thoughtfully.

Megan was silent. She couldn't help but agree with what Darrow had just said, and it worried her that her son showed the same determination and ruthlessness that his father had—he was determined to succeed at any cost.

'The point is that he is liable to take risks.' Megan's eyes widened with fear, but Darrow was quick to reassure her. 'Not that that is anything to worry about in itself— it shows character—but he needs careful watching so that he doesn't do anything too dangerous.'

The fleeting glow of pride that Megan had felt when Darrow had thought her son had character faded instantly.

'You make him sound irresponsible,' she protested angrily.

'Look, Megan,' snapped back Darrow, 'this isn't something I'm prepared to argue about. Most parents are only too glad to have their children properly supervised. It allows them a little free time and their children gain confidence and independence in a safe environment.'

Megan opened her mouth, but Darrow hadn't finished yet. He was determined to make his views known and was not prepared to listen to Megan.

'You hover around him like a broody hen. Maybe he's trying to prove to you that he's not a little boy any more.'

'How dare you?' stormed Megan. But she knew his words were uncannily accurate, and that hurt. 'Since when have you been such an expert on children?' she threw back at him.

'You'd be surprised how much I do know,' he countered swiftly, with an authority that incensed her even further. Yet she knew it wasn't an idle boast; she remembered that he had been a camp counsellor in America.

'Well, whatever you know,' she exclaimed, no longer feeling as confident, 'you don't know Luke. So I'd thank you to keep your opinions to yourself.'

'I can't promise that, Megan,' he said quietly. 'And I always keep my promises,' he added, the cruel gibe causing an instant response from Megan.

'What do you mean by that?' she demanded, fully realising that he was referring to their past again.

The cold expression on his face confirmed what she had thought. 'If Luke wants to participate in the activities available he will have to respect my authority, and if you have a problem with that then I'm afraid I shall have to refuse him access to all the sporting facilities.'

Megan stared hard at Darrow, hating him with a depth that surprised even herself. She remained silent, too angry even to speak. He was taking over. Suddenly Luke had become his responsibility, even though he was unaware that Luke was his son. That hurt—hurt Megan deeply. Part of her so desperately wanted this holiday to be a success, but Darrow seemed equally determined to have his way, and Megan knew she had no alternative but to agree. Darrow was in no humour to give any quarter. She could tell that by the tightness of his stubborn jaw.

'Well, Megan?' he queried impatiently, his eyes cool and assessing as he waited for her reply. 'Do you agree to my terms? Which, I should add, include your exclusion,' he finished, unable to keep the ring of triumph from his tone. He knew he was in total control and seemed to delight in the power he had over her.

'Is there an alternative?' asked Megan, her voice heavy with sarcasm.

'You could leave.'

'We'll stay,' snapped Megan, determined not to be bullied by him.

'So you agree? I want a firm answer, Megan. I know how quickly you change your mind,' he added, with a touch of venom in his tone, and Megan's eyes flew to his, outraged at his attitude. A classic case of the pot calling the kettle, she thought indignantly.

'Yes—yes, I agree,' she spat through her clenched teeth, and she felt the heat of embarrassment cover her cheeks.

'Then I suggest you leave. Now,' he snapped back. His glance briefly flicked to his watch, then back to Megan's face. 'This lesson has another half-hour to go. I'll tell Luke to meet you back at the lodge,' he informed her crisply.

For a moment Megan stared at him, then she turned smartly around and marched away, her steps swift, her whole body stiff with frustrated anger.

CHAPTER FIVE

MEGAN looked around the neat garden with a smile. Faintly in the distance she could hear the gentle trickle of water that acted as a balm on her troubled soul. This meeting hadn't been easy. She had noticed the flicker of disappointment on Janet's face when she'd told her Luke was not with her, but she refused to reason out why she should have been so disappointed. That would be far too dangerous.

Megan silently congratulated herself. She had managed to keep conversation flowing without difficulty. She had kept to safe, neutral subjects, deftly avoiding any questions that came too near the truth, but there was a sparkle in Janet's intelligent grey eyes that quite unnerved her.

'He's the image of his father,' Janet said idly as she'd stirred her tea with a smooth, graceful action.

Megan felt a chill cover her body. The cup of tea she was lifting to her mouth stopped in mid-flight. 'Who?' she asked, forcing her voice to be light and casual, though her hand trembled slightly.

'Luke.'

Megan quickly took a mouthful of tea, to wet her suddenly dry mouth. She had been expecting this, dreading the moment, hoping her denial would be convincing enough. But doubts already assailed her.

'You remember Karl, then?' she asked, her voice overbright and friendly.

Janet gave a short, hard laugh, her mouth creasing into

a strained smile as she fixed her steel-grey eyes on Megan's startled face.

'I'm not blind, Megan. I mean, Luke is the image of Darrow—surely you see it?' she questioned, her tone brooking no argument. She was sure. The steel in her voice, the amusement on her face only reinforced her conviction. Megan felt the blood in her body chill as her whole body iced over. Her cup rattled noisily on the saucer, but failed to drown out the deafening beat of her heart that ran through her ears.

'Janet—' she gave a brief laugh that never fully developed '—what a peculiar thing to say.'

Janet's smile remained the same, her composure not in the least ruffled as she studied Megan carefully. She reached out affectionately and rested her warm hand over Megan's cold one which hung limply in her lap.

'I saw it the moment he came into the room—his stance, his manners, every action, every movement screams Darrow. Surely you know that?' she said, rising to her feet, leaving Megan stunned, unable to deny her son his father any longer.

Janet returned moments later with a large leather-bound book. She opened it and placed it before Megan, resting it on her trembling knees. There was Luke staring out at her—the same clear blue eyes, the same-shaped face, the confident smile. Except it wasn't Luke, it was Darrow—and the likeness was undeniable.

'I checked myself, the moment I came home. I was sure, but—'

'Does Darrow know?' Megan cut in, hating the thrill of excitement in Janet's voice because she knew the problems it would create and yet grateful that at last she had someone to share her secret with. Now her mother had died Megan felt she was carrying her burden alone, and the weight was threatening to overwhelm her.

'No,' Janet replied briefly, then added carefully, 'Not yet.'

'You'll tell him?' Her question was unnecessary, her voice hollow and dead. She knew that Janet would see it as her son's right, and hers as a grandparent, to know Luke—to see him and learn about him, perhaps make up for all those lost years.

'No,' said Janet softly, shaking her head. 'You will.' Her voice was firm and determined, though not lacking in understanding.

'I can't,' Megan pleaded desperately. 'You don't understand.' Her mind was in a turmoil, her head beginning to ache as she thought of the repercussions and the effect all this would have on Luke. She had to protect him at all costs. He was the most important person involved in this terrible family problem.

'He has a right to know,' argued Janet, equally determined. Both women were fighting for their son, each one totally convinced she was doing the right thing.

'He's no rights—none at all,' flared Megan with a sudden burst of outrage. He had betrayed her, rejected her love and her son. Any rights he might have had had certainly been forfeited a long time ago.

'Megan,' said Janet, hearing the pain and fear in Megan's voice and responding to it. 'He must be told. You can't keep it a secret,' she added softly, resting her hands on hers, trying to comfort her.

'Mother!'

It was Darrow, and Megan's eyes flew to Janet's pleadingly, her heart racing as she searched for some compassion. It was out of her hands. Someone else was now in control of her destiny. Megan felt powerless, and more frightened than she had ever done in her life.

'You won't tell him,' she whispered, her voice dry and laced with fear. But she received no reply, because at that moment Darrow entered.

Megan swallowed the pain that crushed against her heart when she saw him. It could have been so different, if only he had kept his promise. But America and his dreams of being a writer had gone far beyond the teenage love he'd had for her, she thought bitterly.

'Darrow.' His mother smiled as he entered. 'Tea?' she offered, picking up the teapot and failing to acknowledge the plea that shone in Megan's eyes.

Darrow hid his surprise at seeing Megan there with deliberate ease, keeping any feelings under tight control. He glanced down at the photo album, a flicker of confusion registering briefly on his face. Megan immediately spotted it and she snapped the book closed to prevent him seeing the pictures.

'Just remembering old times,' she said breathlessly, a faint smile touching the corners of her mouth. He took his cup of tea from his mother with a nod of thanks.

'It's ages since I looked through that album,' he said, settling himself back in his chair and stretching out his long legs. Totally at ease, in direct contrast to Megan, he reached out for the book and Megan's heart sank. She darted a look of sheer panic at Janet, who moved with skilled speed, whipping the book smartly away.

'I've bored Megan enough for one day.' She smiled sweetly at Megan, who flashed her a look of gratitude for her kindness.

Janet went back indoors with the album, leaving Darrow and Megan alone in the garden, where they had whiled away many a summer's day, lost in the mutual silence of each other's love. How times have changed, mused Megan, dragging herself back to the present day as she realised Darrow was talking to her.

'How's the house-clearing going?' he asked as he helped himself to a large piece of home-made shortbread.

'Nearly finished,' admitted Megan almost sadly, brushing from her face the hair which a gentle breeze had blown there. She hated this polite conversation.

'It's hardly been a holiday for you,' he remarked coolly, snapping the yellow shortbread in a clean break, and Megan watched the crumbs fall on to the pure white bone-china plate with interest. Anything to avoid the searching gaze of his eyes.

'It's been a change,' she remarked, not wanting him to see her weakness. He had spoiled the holiday for her by taking total control of Luke. What made it even worse was that Luke seemed thoroughly to enjoy the discipline and to respond to Darrow's wishes with an ease that left Megan speechless.

'Still, you should have a rest—a day off,' he said lightly, but she knew his eyes were still on her. She could feel them searching her the way they always had when he had known she was secretly unhappy.

'Maybe I will,' she said, raising her head to prove to him—or herself—that she had nothing to hide. 'A walk, perhaps,' she added, by way of a suggestion.

'I mean a proper day off.'

Megan looked directly at him. There was something in his tone, a concern she had not expected to hear—not after all this time. They had both changed, done other things, been other places, and yet when she looked at him he still seemed the same. She took in the firm square jaw, the deep set of his clear blue eyes which were emphasised by the perfectly arched dark brows. But beyond the physical was the unspoken current of strength born of suffering. A power that he had not possessed before was now carefully drawn into every feature of his face—part of his character that she had not known.

'Come out on the lake with me?' The offer fell somewhere between an invitation and a command, leaving Megan stunned. How did she feel about this? Grateful or resentful? She couldn't decide. She really didn't want to think about him this much, but his very presence seemed to demand a response from her.

'That's very kind of you—' she began, deciding on a polite but firm rejection. It might be her only chance of survival. She knew that she would be weak compared with the strength he now possessed.

'Not at all,' he effectively cut in, not allowing her refusal the chance to flourish. 'I've a day off tomorrow and need to get away from here, where no one can reach me—like the centre of the lake. Come on, Meggie,' he cajoled, sensing her reluctance. 'It's a simple invitation,' he reassured her. But there was a definite interest and hunger in his eyes that made Megan feel wary.

'OK...' she began hesitantly, but suddenly it seemed like a good idea—the perfect relaxing spot to tell him about Luke. 'Yes—yes, I'd love to,' she agreed enthusiastically, and warmed under the brilliance of the smile he gave her when she accepted.

'Good. I'll bring a picnic lunch. Luke can come too,' he added, with an even wider smile, as if his presence would be a bonus instead of the way other men had viewed her son—tolerating him at best or totally rejecting him. Perhaps he already knew, mused Megan. But she knew that was wrong. He couldn't possibly know. She could imagine his fury when he did find out, and new doubts began to surface.

'I think he's busy tomorrow,' she said. He had been busy most days and though she had missed him dreadfully the change in him was worth any price. He was looking so much better and his confidence was returning; she could tell that by his attitude—so much like his father's.

'Doing what?'

'I'm not sure.' Megan frowned, disliking the curt tone that Darrow had suddenly taken on, sensing an undercurrent of disapproval again and immediately becoming defensive.

'So it's just the two of us, then?' Darrow asked, his eyes dancing with an unspoken invitation that made Megan's stomach contract and her pulse race.

This was the last thing she wanted. Not this—not now. She was too mature, too adult to play silly sexual games with flirtatious behaviour and words laced with innuendo. She couldn't allow herself to feel anything for this man, not even sexual attraction.

But that was hard. He still stirred in her all the passion that he had first awakened in her all those years ago, and Megan was no longer sure whether she was any more immune to him now than she had been then.

Megan awoke early, an undeniable excitement spiralling through her body, an excitement so like all the other times when she had been going out with Darrow. She slipped from her bed and drew back the curtains, allowing the pale early morning light to flood the room. The lake was still, a smooth mirror of water, but a steady strong breeze was rushing through the trees, making it an ideal day for sailing. She could imagine the type of craft Darrow owned, large and classic more than flash, a complete contrast to the tiny rowing-boat they had used to go out on the lake in.

Megan knew exactly what she was going to wear. She had brought with her a neatly tailored navy blazer, and a navy blue and white striped T-shirt matched it perfectly, making a very nautical outfit. She pulled them from her wardrobe, along with a classic-cut pair of stone-washed jeans and a pair of flat navy loafers.

She took a refreshing shower and washed her hair, applying a generous amount of almond-scented conditioner. She towelled herself dry, wrapped her hair neatly into a turban and went to the kitchen. Suddenly she really felt as if she was on holiday, and she wanted to treat herself to a cooked breakfast that she could share with Luke.

She flicked on a cassette, and gentle music filled the silence of the early morning. She poured herself a glass of fresh grapefruit juice and took a large mouthful, grimacing at the sharp, tangy flavour. She began to make breakfast, setting the table outside on the balcony so that they could enjoy the wonderful view. Luke was quite happy at being awoken early, which surprised Megan because normally he was reluctant to get out of bed.

'Well, what are you doing today?' Megan asked as she looked with delight at the hungry assault her son was making on his breakfast. It was so good to see his appetite returning to his insatiable normal. She hoped he had something planned. She hated the thought of leaving him to his own devices as it was supposed to be *their* holiday, a shared experience.

'I've plans,' Luke answered non-committally, then added as he caught the look of concern shadowing his mother's face, 'I'll be fine. You go and enjoy yourself.'

'Are you sure?' Megan persisted, still doubtful, and a

niggling suspicion formed at the back of her mind, troubling her but not taking on any definite form.

'Yes,' Luke snapped, a flare of annoyance lighting his eyes briefly. 'I've told you, I've other plans,' he said, pushing away his plate and Megan's questions at the same time.

'All right.' Megan smiled quickly, not wanting an argument to develop and mar her day. A sudden rap on the door made her heart leap. 'It's Darrow,' she said, trying to suffocate the twirl of excitement that swept over her. She was not a silly teenager with a crush, but somehow that was exactly how she felt.

'I'm not ready,' she gasped, almost breathless, clutching her silk robe around her body. 'Let him in while I get dressed,' she told Luke as she rushed back to her bedroom and began to dress with nervous, agitated fingers. She was ready in record time and hurried back, stopping at the door as she caught the atmosphere between them. Her eyes darted from the grim expression on Darrow's face to Luke's pinkened cheeks.

'What's the matter?' she asked nervously, her heart sinking as she realised there had been friction between them again. the atmosphere and freezing silence were the obvious tell-tale signs.

'Nothing,' clipped Darrow, his eyes still fixed on Luke in quiet warning.

'Luke?' she asked, turning her attention on her son. He was struggling with his emotions, she could see that, and she was determined to get to the bottom of this trouble.

'Nothing,' he said, his tone dull and sullen, and he raised his eyes briefly to look at Darrow, as if wondering whether he had said the right thing.

Megan sighed loudly. She hated this. She was torn between the two of them, her heart being wrenched every time they argued, and she wondered whether or not it would always be like this, even if either of them found out the truth.

'What is it?' she demanded. She wanted to be a peace-maker, to bring them closer together, though she didn't question herself as to why.

'But I could do it,' insisted Luke, his temper growing rapidly when faced with such a brick wall. He was not used to such inflexibility. Megan was easily persuaded once faced with any resentment from him.

'No,' snapped Darrow, his voice sharp and cutting, then he added in a gentler tone, 'Luke, you haven't the stamina or skill, besides—'

'I could,' interrupted Luke sharply, his cheeks glowing with immature temper, and he sank his hands deeper into his pockets, looking at Darrow resentfully. 'You just won't give me the chance. The others want me to go.'

'Do they?' growled Darrow, his eyes narrowing, and Megan felt sure he would have something to say to the group concerned as his expression had grown even stonier. 'Well, that's academic, because you're not going.'

'Come with us,' pleaded Megan, joining in, trying to pacify them both as she saw their tempers mounting with every word. She felt trapped, understanding both points of view and knowing them both well enough to see that neither one of them would be willing to compromise. 'Come on, Luke, it will be fun,' she cajoled. But her pleas fell on deaf ears.

'No, I don't want to,' he replied sulkily, his toe stub-bing into the carpet, making a furrow in the pile. Dar-row's eyebrows rose in mockery at his childish behav-iour. 'I'm going out,' he stormed as he realised the delight his action was giving Darrow, and he pulled at

the door so that it slammed noisily and the lodge reverberated with the impact.

Megan sighed audibly and sank back into a chair. She
had never seen Luke so upset and it distressed her
greatly. How was she going to cope with him if this was
the way he was going to behave? The thought worried
her. He was growing up all the time, and she could see
that the way ahead would be difficult.

'I don't think I should go now. I wouldn't enjoy it,'
she said by way of explanation. 'I really think I should
stay,' she added, shrugging off her blazer—till Darrow
stopped her.

'No,' he told her firmly, pulling her blazer back on to
her shoulders. 'You have not had a moment's rest since
you arrived. This is your first chance of a day out and
nothing is going to stop you. Besides, it will do him good
to learn that he can't always do what he wants.'

'I just don't want to spoil his holiday,' insisted Megan,
still not sure, but she had been so looking forward to
going that it seemed wrong not to.

'I would,' Darrow said thoughtfully, sinking on to the
arm of Megan's chair. 'Megan, Luke is growing up. I
think spoiling his holiday will be better in the long run,
because if you carry on giving in to him you may spoil
him for life.' His voice was controlled, his argument
sound, but Megan hated the criticism of her son, and the
implied criticism of the way she was bringing him up.
She resented the fact that he was offering his opinion
when she held him partly responsible for the argument.

Darrow wanted to be part of the problems she was
having now, but where had he been when Luke was
frightened of the dark, suffering from mumps? Where
had he been when Luke swam for the first time or took
his first step, read his first book? That was the loneliness

of a one-parent family—sadness or joy, it made no difference. There was still no one to share it with, no one who could care as much for your child as you did.

'You're letting the others go—can't you see, it's just not fair?' she challenged, suddenly hating him for missing all those other moments that they could have shared. Turning to face him, Megan suddenly realised how close he was—too close. Their faces were only inches apart; she could feel his warm breath on her face, see the deep blue of his irises. She swallowed the dry lump in her throat, her own eyes dilating in response, and her pulse increased its rate till her blood seemed to thunder through her body.

'I've already explained; he hasn't the stamina or the experience,' Darrow repeated patiently, trying to ignore the sharpness in her tone, the brightness that glowed in the deep pools of her normally cool green eyes.

'That's your opinion,' she snapped back, knowing there was more than an element of truth in his words, and that only hurt her all the more.

Luke's illness had been another crisis she had had to face alone as a single parent. All the pain and fear of those early days, when Luke had first been taken into hospital, came back to her with overwhelming clarity— the sense of isolation, the dread that he might have some terrible illness that they would not be able to cure. But thankfully he was all right, and now all Megan wanted was to put the past behind her, to bury the knowledge that he was not fully well so that they could both get on with their lives. Coming here had been supposed to do that. Not only to build their troubled relationship, but to help Luke become strong and confident again, and Darrow was stopping him, reminding both her and Luke of his apparent weaknesses, and that cut her deeply.

'Yes, it is my opinion,' he told her flatly, seeing her disappointment in him shining in her eyes, reflected in her expression. The troubled look held a secret that he knew she was not prepared to share. 'And it's my opinion that counts round here, and Luke had better get used to it,' he ended, with an assurance that only irritated her all the more. Besides, there had been a message in his words that she immediately responded to.

Megan looked up at him, her brow furrowed, tension pulling at every nerve in her body as she struggled to remain calm, unaffected by his words, though her breath was shallow—almost painful.

'Why?' asked Megan. One word that forced him to explain what he meant and gave him no place to hide.

'Because otherwise it could make it difficult for us,' he murmured softly, his head moving slightly to the side as he rested his eyes on her, studying her reaction to his words. Immediately Megan tore her gaze from his face.

'There is no ''us'', Darrow,' she said firmly, desperately hiding the impact his words had made on her. 'I'm just here on holiday,' she continued, with a coolness that amazed even herself. The smile on his face spread, showing the gleaming row of white teeth against his outdoor tan as if he was mocking her words and the suggestion that she was here just for a holiday. 'Let's just enjoy today, shall we?' she added hopefully. She wanted to make him understand that there was no future between them—could never be, not now.

'OK. Let's go,' he agreed, too readily, and Megan knew that it would be a topic he would return to.

Darrow had always been confident, sure of himself in a way that unnerved Megan. He had been the same about his writing—the knowledge that he would succeed had always been a reality to him, his scholarship in America always just around the corner. It had been that self-assurance, that commitment to write and travel which had made it impossible for Megan to tell him the truth all those years ago.

Darrow saw her falter, lost in her own very private thoughts, and misread them. 'Luke will be all right,' he reassured her, with a winning smile that touched the very core of her.

'You sound certain,' she stated, with a mocking inflexion to her tone, and he guessed that she meant it as a criticism.

'I am, but only because I've made sure Joe is going to keep an eye on him,' he explained.

'You knew he wouldn't come with us? How?'

'I've had plenty of experience,' he answered with a cryptic look that fuelled her curiosity with a measure of alarm and disappointment. Did he have other children? He had not married, but children were still a real possibility, and that hurt.

'Personal experience?' she gibed, letting a bitter sarcasm coat her words, and she saw him stiffen with anger as his jaw flexed.

He closed the door behind them and offered his hand to help her down the steep, rocky path that led to the marina. He stopped for a moment at the top, his eyes scanning the distant shore and a smile touching his lips as he raised his hand and pointed, far away into the distance. Megan followed his finger, her eyes screwed up against the brightness of the day as she tried to focus on his point of interest.

'See that row of barrack buildings on the furthest shore?' he said, a definable pride in his tone as he cast her a swift glance before returning his gaze to the buildings.

'Yes, I see them.' Megan nodded. They were a new addition since her day, and despite being modern buildings they fitted into the raw scenery very well. They were made from huge logs, their roofs tiled in green, and the huge solar windows the only concession to modern living.

'It's a project of mine to help inner-city children,' he explained as they began their descent. Megan was aware of his tightening grip; the ground was loose and she could so easily have slipped. 'Youngsters aged between nine and eighteen years come here and have the opportunity to experience a totally different lifestyle and gain some independence, some sense of responsibility.'

'And it was those boys Luke wanted to go with today,' Megan stated calmly, the sudden realisation coming over her. Luke would want to prove himself, just like his father, confident always in his own ability.

'That's right, and believe me he wouldn't have survived. They're a real tough bunch—some already have a criminal record. They need firm handling,' he concluded grimly, a wry smile touching his lips, and Megan could see that he had a definite respect for these less fortunate children. Hadn't he always? she mused, thinking back to her own childhood. Maybe that was how he had seen her—a poor little waif who needed help.

She cast him a covert glance, but he gave no indication of his thoughts; he just smiled, his eyes alive with the sparkle she'd thought he had lost forever, and it stirred emotions deep within her—emotions she was sure must remain deeply buried.

'That's my craft,' he said as they reached the lake, the laughter bubbling up as he saw her face.

'You're joking.' Megan grinned in response, already knowing he wasn't, and the careful lock she had kept on her emotions was slowly being unlocked by his calcu-lated actions.

'What did you expect?' he asked. 'Something grander?'

'A lot grander—still, I think this is ideal,' she was forced to admit, looking at the tiny rowing-boat as it bobbed in the water. 'It's not the same one, surely?' she asked, unable to believe that the tiny boat which had given them so much pleasure had survived.

'Yes—same one. I've had it overhauled, but the name is the same,' he said gently, pointing to the name so carefully and freshly painted on the side, and Megan gave an inaudible gasp as she read the familiar name.

'*Love's Haven*,' she said out loud, her tone wistful. It was ironic that this little boat, a symbol of their love, should have survived the storms of life when their love had fallen at the first hurdle.

'Untie her, then,' called Darrow, breaking into her thoughts as he jumped inside, his hand outstretched towards her, and Megan, with familiar ease, accepted it graciously.

Frozen, the pair of them were locked for the briefest of moments in the past, memories rushing up and sweep-ing over them, breaking down the barriers of the past. Megan stepped aboard. Heedless of the rocking, they re-mained standing, looking at one another as the years fell away, leaving them both exposed to a fresh wave of emo-tion. Neither of them spoke. Words were unnecessary, an intrusion on the powerful feelings that forced them both into action, and like a well-rehearsed ballet they moved together.

'I can't believe this is happening,' he whispered, his breath warm against her ear as he began to plant a series of warm kisses over her neck and face, moving skilfully to her softly parted lips.

Megan felt a slow shiver race through her body as all the untapped passion she knew she possessed was stirred back into springtime awareness. He had always been able to ignite her by the slightest touch. She felt his hand wrap around her body, and her own mirrored his as she clasped him to her. Everything quickened. It was too long that they had been together and not delighted in the very taste of each other.

She leaned into him, letting him feel the weight of her body, delighting in the sense of his strong body against hers as the intensity of their kisses increased. It was madness, but she didn't care. She hadn't realised how much she still cared; how much of her still wanted him. Her mouth explored his, enjoying the well-remembered contours of his lips, the shape of his body as they moulded together. The boat rocked in protest and they were forced to draw back, to steady themselves. His arm stayed hugged around her waist, her hands resting gently on his shoulders, and the desire they had aroused in each other shone from their eyes. Neither one of them could conceal it.

The cool breeze from the lake suddenly felt quite chilling against the heat they had aroused in each other.

'Perhaps we'd better set off,' Darrow said, smiling lightly. Megan nodded in silent agreement as she moved to sit down, watching him now with a new, fully alive awareness that she was still at pains to conceal. 'Careful,' he said, his arm tightening in support as she lost her balance. 'Are you all right?' he asked quickly as she sat down.

'Yes, fine,' she lied, her heart thudding with the memory of the events that had just taken place. She lifted her gaze to stare out across the lake. The place had not changed, her emotions to Darrow had not changed—everything was as it always had been. But now there was Luke, and Megan knew that despite how she felt he had to come first.

'Are you sure you're all right, Meggie?' Darrow persisted as he took up the oars in his strong hands. His eyes had never left her face. He was searching her soul for any signs of doubt.

'I'm fine.' She smiled, forcing a lightness into her voice. He nodded silently as he turned his head and began to manoeuvre the boat out into the deeper waters, and Megan knew that he hadn't believed her for one moment.

CHAPTER SIX

MEGAN gripped the edge of the bench she was perched on as the boat bobbed and dipped its way out into the lake. She watched Darrow as he pulled back the oars, the muscles in his arms rippling with each smooth movement. Megan let a gentle sigh escape her lips as she began to relax. She lowered her hand into the water at the side of the boat and let it hang there in an attempt to soothe the heat that coursed through her body. It cut a ripple through the water which she watched with childlike fascination.

She hadn't expected to be kissed, and certainly not to kiss back, but at the time it had all seemed so perfectly natural, the intimacy that had sprung up between them a spontaneous reaction to the desire they both felt but had managed to control. Megan didn't want to speak. Voices would have destroyed the beautiful intimacy of silence. Words had ceased to have any meaning and would only have detracted from the depth of feeling they both were experiencing.

The sky was slowly clearing, the mists ascending into the sky, revealing the full colour and beauty of the hills. It was an idyllic day.

'You can see the accommodation for the boys better now,' Darrow said, breaking the silence as he brought the boat to a standstill and pointed over to the bank. Megan followed his outstretched hand and looked with interest at the neat row of log chalets that dotted the bank, nestling between the dark green trees.

'Aren't you taking a risk, having them here?' she asked dubiously, suddenly feeling grateful that Luke had not gone with them. She wasn't sure if they were the type of people she wanted him to mix with—he could be easily influenced.

'They're a good bunch of kids, really,' Darrow explained, picking up the oars again. 'But like I say, give them an inch and they'll take a mile—especially the teenage boys,' he added with a knowing grin, and Megan smiled in mutual acknowledgement.

'Don't I know it?' she agreed, lifting her hand from the lake, shaking the water from her wet fingers. The drops fell in an arc of diamond balls that caught the brightness of the daylight, but her action did not conceal the underlying tension in her voice.

'Boys of that age are just beginning to understand the strength and power they have. They're young men and want everyone to know it. Here they can stretch themselves fully, but within parameters or they soon lose their direction.'

'So your word is sacrosanct?'

'It has to be, but that doesn't mean I don't have problems now and again. None of them are angels.'

'So how do you handle them?' Megan asked, intrigued. She thought of her own attempts with Luke, but if anything she only made matters worse, and even the slightest incident seemed to develop into a full-scale row. Darrow paused, resting his arms over the smooth wooden oars, and looked at her closely, understanding the dilemma she was facing.

'I'm firm but fair, and few are foolish enough to cross me a second time,' he said seriously, a spark glittering in his lambent eyes.

Megan nodded silently in agreement. She couldn't

imagine anyone foolish enough to cross Darrow—he had
a formidable temper which, once provoked, took a great
deal of time to subside. A breeze blew across the lake,
stirring her hair, and she raised her hand to smooth it
back into place as a wave of guilt came over her. He
would have been a good father too. Often, recently, she
had caught the sense of longing in Luke when he had
spoken of Darrow—longing for the father he had been
denied.

'It's been a long time since I've been out in a boat,'
she mused softly, half to herself, as she closed her eyes
and lifted her head to the sky, allowing the sun to heat
her face.

'Too long, Meggie. April the seventeenth, to be exact,'
he told her, the warmth in his voice alerting her. She
knew the date well. She knew every day, every date they
had spent together. Each one was imprinted indelibly on
her mind, but she couldn't afford to let him know how
much he had meant to her.

'Was it?' she asked casually, but even now she could
still feel the piece of paper confirming her pregnancy as
she had screwed it up in her hand till her nails had dug
into the soft flesh of her palm. April the seventeenth
would always stand out as a date to remember in her
emotional diary. That was the day he had told her he was
leaving, and she had known she had no right to keep him
there, even if she was carrying his child. She had loved
him too much to use that type of blackmail, and besides,
then she had been so confident that he would return.

'You haven't changed. You look exactly the same.
See, you still have a row of freckles across the bridge of
your nose.' He laughed, tracing his long fingers in a gentle sweep across the familiar map of her features. Megan's eyes shot open and she shifted in her seat to a more

upright position. He had taken advantage of her youth all those years ago and she was not about to let him do it again.

'We've both changed, Darrow. You can't turn the clock back, much as we both might like to,' she explained, half of her wanting to, half of her too afraid. She had loved him once before, and she knew it wouldn't be that hard for her to love him again.

'Can't we, Megan?' He took her hand in his, forcing her eyes to meet his and see the banked desire and hope there. 'Just for today,' he murmured wistfully, 'let's turn the clock back.'

'The idea is very appealing,' she was forced to admit as recollections almost overwhelmed her.

'Please, Meggie.'

'For today.' She nodded, suffocating the cries of doubt that tried to take over her reasoning. This was too easy, too simple. But she dismissed her thoughts, determined to play the game, even if only for today.

'Before we do, though, can I ask you a question?'

Her gaze narrowed as deep chills invaded her body, but she met his eyes head-on, fixing a smile to her face that hid the fear that raged inside.

'Of course not. You already know my age and what other secret could a woman want to keep?' She laughed, hoping he would catch the mood and stop looking so serious, though she knew that her age wasn't her most precious secret.

'Your marriage was happy?'

'I thought we were forgetting all that, just for today,' she countered swiftly, still keeping her voice light and joky, but her heart skipped a beat at the question. She wondered what had prompted it—mild curiosity, or a deeper emotion? Maybe even jealousy?

'I just wanted to know, seeing as fate seemed to come between us.'

Fate. The word screamed through her mind. Fate, she thought angrily. Fate under the name of Carrie. Hardly fate, more his own weakness, she thought, too angry to speak for a moment. Then, swallowing her rage and disappointment, she answered him.

'We were happy for the short time we were together,' she said, enjoying the look of disappointment that flickered in his eyes. What had he expected? Her to pine away while he made a new life for himself with a new love?

'Surely your life in America was far more exciting?' she goaded, not fully understanding her motivation. Did she really want him to tell her about Carrie, the girl he had given everything up for—including his precious writing? She felt so angry with herself, and with him, for all the shattered dreams. The boat was still as he laid his oars down and leant forward, resting his arms on his knees.

'Well, my American dream turned out to be something of a nightmare,' he said bitterly, the light in his eyes darkening as he spoke, which intrigued Megan even more.

She lifted her chin, tilting her head back, her eyes squinting in the brightness of the sun. She did not want to give him the satisfaction of knowing that she cared, but she had to know, had to have at least some knowledge of why he had so easily given up the ambition that had driven them apart.

'Care to elaborate?' Her curiosity got the better of her. She saw the flicker of doubt in his eyes, a troubled, disturbed look that cast a dark shadow over his face. 'As I recall, it was your success in America that brought you all this,' she said, waving her arm in an arching sweep, taking in the whole area.

'True,' he conceded, almost reluctantly. 'But I paid a high price.' The deep pain in his voice threatened to overwhelm her and she felt that he was miles away from her, locked in his past, which she was not a part of, and that hurt.

'You mean you sold your literary soul writing soap operas?' she joked, forcing laughter into her voice as she tried to drive away the dark shadows that were welling up between them.

'I lost more than that in America,' he said grimly, his voice strained with emotion. He moved slightly towards her, but it was enough. Megan was not sure where the source of his pain originated, but it wasn't important now. All she wanted to do was to hold him. To chase away the past and to rid them both of the pain and hurt that they both felt. Maybe now was the right time for healing, for forgetting the past and just living for the present.

She moved too, curling herself into his outstretched arms. She sat down on the floor of the boat between his legs, her back resting on him and his arms settling on her shoulders. She lifted her hand, stroking the back of his hand with a gentle touch, enjoying the feel of his skin against her fingers. Neither of them spoke. She knew there was something he was not telling her, a secret that was too painful to share, and she wondered whose feelings he was considering. It was all so natural, sitting there, the boat rocking gently in the waters, just like old times.

'What was America like?' she said dreamily as she closed her eyes in an attempt to shut out the past.

'It was all right.'

'You don't sound too enthusiastic,' she joked, hiding her hurt as she remembered how much she had struggled in allowing him to have his dream.

'No, it was good—different from here. The weather, for a start.' She could sense he was grinning and a smile curled her soft mouth. 'It was hot—humid even. And the pace of life—so fast.'

'I should have thought that would suit you.'

He had always been the high-flyer. His ambition had known no bounds then—he had been so self-assured, so confident. It was all those things that had made Megan feel she was not able to compete. She had felt that telling him they were to have a child would have been like a millstone wrapped round his neck, weighing him down. She had loved him too much to do that, and besides, she had always admired and respected his talent. He had a natural gift for writing that she was sure America would develop fully—a gift to share with the world—and she could not have denied the world his skill.

'It did at first,' he admitted, and Megan allowed herself a moment of self-congratulation. She had been right; the high life had suited him.

'And you managed a measure of success.' She knew that writing a television series would not have been his first choice, but even so it had been extremely popular, its success lying in the fact that the characters were so skilfully drawn.

'Oh, yes,' he sighed, expelling the air from his lungs noisily. 'I've a lot to thank America for.'

'I detect a 'but' there,' said Megan, turning round so she could face him. She read the confusion in the dark depths of his eyes as he struggled to think something through. He faltered, as if he was about to tell her something, and Megan's breath caught in her throat, but he smiled instead.

'Well, there's no place like home.' He ran his hand down over her hair, his fingers resting momentarily under her chin. 'And you, Meggie?' he asked, his eyes fixed on hers, trapping her. 'How did you cope bringing up a child alone? It can't have been easy.'

'I coped,' she stated simply, the words almost catching in her throat as she thought of the times she hadn't. The times her mother had so willingly come to the rescue, saving her from drowning under the weight of single responsibility.

'You did well. He's a fine lad.'

She couldn't let him see the effect his words had on her—a strange cocktail of emotions, pride mingled with the fine thread of anger.

'Yes—yes, he is. I'm very proud of him,' she admitted, her face as tranquil as the waters they were floating on.

'You should be. I can see he's a little headstrong, but they all are at that age.'

'Don't I know it?' sighed Megan, raising her eyebrows to heaven in mock-horror. They both laughed—warm, genuine laughter that rippled over the water, filling the air.

'But you've coped admirably since Karl died,' he said, and Megan stiffened, a death-chill cooling her body. She always felt fearful whenever Karl was mentioned. She was so afraid of making some terrible slip that would reveal the truth.

'Yes, my business seems to be doing well at the moment.' She smiled, waving a pair of crossed fingers at him for luck. She could see the swift look of surprise, quickly replaced with one of admiration.

'Despite the recession?' he asked, obviously intrigued.

'Not too bad. It's a small health club—nothing grand, just a well-stocked gym, two rooms for exercise classes, some showers and a solarium. It needs more investment, really.'

'And you run it alone—no partner?'

'A partner—no. Help—yes. I began to take an exercise class after having Luke—to keep myself trim.' She laughed a little self-consciously. 'I've only been able to go it alone in the last year. Up until then I'd just been teaching classes at the local sports centre for the council,' she explained quickly, leaving out the difficulty of working when trying to bring up a child alone. It had not been easy. She had often been shattered, and her wage had been barely enough to cover essentials, but they had survived. And now she hoped all her financial difficulties were in the past.

'And it is successful?'

'Early days yet, but yes, I think it will work. It's for women only, so it's not as competitive as a mixed gym. The women tend to help and encourage each other, unlike men,' she finished ruefully.

'So that's why you look so young,' he murmured huskily, his eyes taking on a slumberous warmth as his gaze roamed possessively over her body, heating the blood that was now racing through her veins.

'Do I?' she teased lightly, raising her face until it was inches from his.

'Of course.' A slow smile creased his face, his voice low yet inviting. She knew she was flirting with him, knew it was a dangerous game, but she was enjoying herself. She suddenly *felt* young again, more free than she had done in years.

'I don't feel fit,' she confessed. 'It's been a difficult year.'

'Maybe this is the turning point for both of us,' he said, his tone measured and controlled. 'A new start,' he added thoughtfully. Megan gave him a half-smile and carefully avoiding answering him. She deftly changed the subject.

'I'm hungry—where's that picnic?' She laughed, moving safely back on to her bench, suddenly eager to put some distance between them as she tried to work out exactly how she felt towards him. Darrow nodded, but his expression warned her that he was aware of her action and would be returning to this conversation later.

They moored up on the far bank, at a sandy area complete with huge rocks left behind after the Ice Age, which afforded them some shelter from the cool breeze that blew in from across the lake.

'Coffee?' he offered, passing Megan a Thermos cup filled with the steaming hot drink. She nodded, accepting it gratefully and wrapping her fingers around the cup, allowing it to warm her hands.

'Perhaps now you're back in Rannaleigh you'll write the novel you always talked about,' Megan said, helping herself to a sandwich.

'I don't think so,' he said, taking a large mouthful of coffee with a gesture that made her think he would have preferred something stronger. 'I've more than enough to do running this place,' he added, but even to Megan's ears it sounded like a poor excuse.

'You can't mean that,' she protested. 'You always said that you wanted to write—needed to write.' She knew her voice had risen, but she was so outraged. His writing had meant everything to him, even more than her; how dared he disregard it now, as if it was of no importance? It made all her sacrifices useless gestures, and that hurt so very deeply.

'I was rather blinkered, wasn't I?' He grinned, but the laughter never reached his eyes. They looked empty, dead, as if he had paid a high price for his ambition. Megan studied his face, searching for the glimmer of enthusiasm that he had always had, but it was no longer there and her heart sank within her. 'I just don't feel like writing any more,' he confessed, the words catching in his throat, as if the admission hurt him more than he was prepared to admit.

'But you must,' insisted Megan, hardly recognising him. It had always been Darrow's reason for living—he had always been writing, always scribbling. 'Such talent—'

'Talent!' cut in Darrow, his bitterness spilling out as he continued, 'A third-rate soap opera. I wouldn't even have done that had it not been for Carrie.' He stopped short, suddenly conscious of the admission he had made, and he dropped his gaze, unable to face the flare of hurt that blazed in Megan's eyes.

For a moment she was lost in a sea of her own unhappiness. Carrie's name on his lips had upset her more than she'd ever thought it would, and now she was struggling to hide the wealth of emotions that were ready to engulf her.

'You must write,' she said finally, ignoring the mention of Carrie. 'It's part of you,' she persisted. She knew how much his writing meant to him even if he seemed to have forgotten.

'I guess you're right,' he said, his voice lacking any real conviction. He glanced upwards. 'Cover your ears,' he told her, and she did automatically as one the latest aircraft flew across. Its speedy passage was over as quickly as a flash of lightning.

'There never used to be this many,' Megan complained, the peace of the day having been momentarily shattered by the roar of the engines.

'Time has moved on. Lots of things have changed. Except you, Megan—never you,' he said, his words taking her by surprise, and he moved closer. It was the perfect moment—the ideal time to tell him.

'Darrow, I want to tell you something,' she began, her voice breathless, a pink tint of colour staining her normally pale complexion and her eyes widening to green pools.

'Confession time?' His breath was warming her face as he drew closer, making the words difficult to form in her mind.

'Yes, something like that,' she admitted self-consciously, her teeth sinking into her lower lip as she nibbled at it in agitation.

'Then no,' he said firmly as he placed his strong fingers over her softly swelling lips. 'The past is gone, Megan, and we can't change it. So let's just forget it for today and enjoy ourselves.'

'I want—'

'No, Meggie,' he insisted, refilling her coffee-cup. 'Today is for us—no one else.'

She nodded in agreement. She would tell him, but not now. Let them savour this moment.

'We used to do this every Sunday, remember?'

'I remember, and you used to try and teach me how to fish.'

'Only as an excuse to put my arms round you.' He laughed as Megan blushed.

Then she retorted with a wide grin, 'It's the only reason I wanted to learn.' She laughed too, her laughter catching in her throat as he took the cup from her hands and pushed her playfully on to the soft, warm sand.

Megan surrendered herself willingly to his expert lips, her hands pulling his shoulders down towards her. Her hands were surprisingly steady as they moved over his back, enjoying remapping the hard, muscular ripples that she knew so well. Their bodies fused closer together, moulding with familiar ease as the intensity of his kisses grew. It was a perfect ending to a perfect day.

CHAPTER SEVEN

THE sun was a red globe of light in a sunset-orange and blue sky as they began their way back over the lake to the marina. They let the silence engulf them; it gave an intimacy to their trip that neither of them wanted to shatter.

Megan turned her head to see what had caught Darrow's eyes, causing him to frown, his eyes narrowing on some point in the distance. For a moment she was taken aback, for there, waiting on the quay, was a large group of people milling around obviously watching for Darrow's return. Megan turned her attention back to Darrow, unable to comprehend what was going on. The cool green pools of her eyes looked at him, serenely unperturbed by the crowd.

'Looks like a welcoming party,' she joked, with a ready smile curling her soft lips, but her light-heartedness was not returned. Darrow's frown seemed to deepen even further, his mouth becoming a thin line of disapproval. His arms pulled back hard on the oars to increase their speed. His muscles rippled the length of his arms with the effort, and a faint sheen of perspiration glistened on his forehead.

'Hardly that,' he mumbled, almost breathless with the exertion of rowing so fast. He kept his eyes firmly on the marina ahead, so deeply troubled that the intimacy of the afternoon they had spent together seemed to have been completely forgotten. Megan couldn't help but wonder if it had meant more to her than it had done to him.

'What's happened?' asked Megan, suddenly bewil-
dered as they drew even closer. The crowd milling
around was generating an unhealthy atmosphere that
seemed to hang in the air, disturbing its tranquillity. The
fear and tension was almost tangible in the muttering of
their voices, and Megan felt her own anxiety levels increase.

'I've no idea what's happened,' snapped back Darrow.
'But it doesn't look good,' he added grimly. His voice
was racked with an inner torment that was finding release
in his short temper. The boat hit the side with a shud-
dering thud and Darrow jumped to his feet, rocking it
still further so that Megan had to grip the sides to retain
her balance.

'What's up, Joe?' he called, throwing the rope to the
sports manager, who began to tie up at once as he answered him, a flash of fear and sorrow reflected in every
crease on his well-worn face.

'I'm sorry, Darrow—' he began huskily, but Darrow
cut in impatiently, his nerves already shredded to a fine
thread that was about to snap irreparably.

'Leave the apologies till later,' he said, already out of
the boat and offering Megan a hand, which she gladly
accepted as she sprang to his side. 'Well?' he said, turning smartly around and fixing his eyes on the now silent
group. 'Give me the facts,' he snapped, his eyes skimming over everyone, hoping to spark a response.

'It's the orienteering group,' volunteered Joe. 'They
returned two hours ago, but one of their group is missing,' he explained hurriedly, waiting for an explosion
from Darrow that never came. Instead he became im-
mobile, locked in his own personal torment. Megan could
sense it, yet knew she was incapable of reaching him. He

was too far lost in his own thoughts, which darkened his eyes with black clouds of despair.

'The Manchester group?' he asked finally, in disbelief. 'They're too experienced,' he muttered, shaking his head in an attempt to rid himself of the thought. It was like a bad dream repeating itself, and all he wanted to do was to wake up.

'That's right, the Manchester group. A fine bunch of lads,' agreed Joe, unaware of the strangeness that seemed to have taken over Darrow.

'That's really odd,' Darrow continued, ignoring Joe's remark. 'It's their third year. I would have thought—'

'He wasn't one of the group,' Joe intervened. He spoke softly, knowing the impact his words would make. There was a world of difference between an experienced person and an amateur lost on the hills. The latter could easily turn into a tragedy, especially if a mist should come down.

'He wasn't?' growled Darrow, suddenly alert. Every muscle in his body was now attuned to the danger, his lambent eyes flaring with a dangerous cocktail of alarm and anger. The calm façade he had worn was now replaced by a look of cold anguish, and his skin paled in horror under his golden tan as Joe continued.

'It was Luke. Luke—Megan's son.' Joe cast a quick, brief look of sympathy at Megan as he spoke. Megan's hand flew to her mouth, but it failed to silence the an-guished cry that escaped from her dry lips. She suddenly felt sick, her body chilled, almost numb, and she gave a shiver as she suddenly became aware of the cool breeze that blew across the lake, icing over her body.

'He attempted to follow them. They told him to go back, but...' Joe's voice trailed away as Darrow began to march towards the centre, already shrugging off his jacket in angry, swift movements.

Megan hurried after him, Joe following at a discreet distance, unwilling to come between them. Darrow slammed into the changing-rooms and sank on to a pine-slatted wooden bench, pulling off his trainers and thin socks, replacing them with a woollen pair of socks and thick walking-boots.

'Where was he last spotted?' he demanded as he tucked his trousers into his boots and began to pull his outdoor waterproofs from the cupboard.

'About two miles from the station, making his way over to the falls,' Joe informed him crisply. It wasn't much to go on, especially if he had no sense of direction, but at least it was something.

'Get a search party...' ordered Darrow, pulling his coat on and standing up, taking a quick glance at his watch. Megan watched his every move, willing him to hurry. Every second counted; she knew that. She had grown up here, knew the terrible consequences of exposure on high ground.

'Kevin has already left with three others,' Joe informed him, already dressed to go with Darrow.

'Right—good. We've a couple of hours before darkness falls, and he's in good health, so he should be OK.' Darrow's voice had taken on the tone of calm authority. His actions were all considered, to instil confidence and calm in the groups going out to search, but Megan was not so easily fooled. She could see the fine tension lines that pulled at his mouth, the fierce alertness in his Prussian blue eyes, and she knew that despite the consequences she had to be honest.

'He—he's not,' she faltered, aware of the silence that

had descended as she spoke. 'He's not well,' she whispered, hardly audible.

'What?' snapped Darrow, pivoting round to glare at her, sparing her none of his anger and disbelief. Megan winced inwardly, but her child's safety was at stake here, so she bore his anger and continued.

'He's been ill with glandular fever,' she explained slowly, and a painful lump swelled in her throat when she thought of him out there, lost and alone.

'Now you tell me,' growled Darrow in exasperation, resentment glittering in his eyes.

'I didn't think it was important,' protested Megan, reacting to the censure in his tone, his anger fuelling her own.

'Not important? Get real! You know damn well it's important. That's why you're telling me now.' The hard line of his mouth thinned as his jaw tensed. 'The effects of glandular fever are long-term. Unusual fatigue can last up to twelve months after. When was he diagnosed?' he demanded sharply, his skin taking on a grey hue under his weather-beaten tan.

Megan flinched at his words; she knew it was true, but Luke had been all right so far.

'He came out of hospital two months ago,' she admitted in a low voice, dropping her eyes so that she would not have to see the fury she knew would be on Darrow's face. She could see how wrong she had been, keeping this information from him, but no one could have envisaged this happening.

'Two months,' he repeated, letting out a low whistle as he zipped up his coat. His every action was now weighed down with yet another problem.

'He's strong,' protested Megan defensively as myriad

doubts filled her mind and hot tears of fear pricked the back of her eyes.

'He'd better be,' Darrow informed her coldly. 'The temperature can drop dramatically up there once the sun sets, and if the mists come down...' He shrugged, sparing her none of the possibilities.

Megan felt that she had to go with them. She pulled at the heavy waterproof coat that was hanging on a hook near the door, losing her arms in the heavy folds as she struggled with agitated hands to find the sleeve.

'What do you think you're doing?' he demanded in a savagely low tone, pulling the coat from her and freezing her to the spot with his icy glare.

'I'm coming with you,' she snapped back, ignoring the tight grip he had on her wrist. Abruptly he released her with a disdainful flick.

'No way.'

'You can't stop me,' Megan bit back, determined to help in the search regardless of how Darrow felt. She couldn't just wait here like some little woman, helpless and useless.

'Can't I?' Darrow threatened softly, his face a ruthless mask that was brooking no argument.

'He's my son.' Megan tried to make her voice sound strong, but it came out like a plea. 'I have to come,' she insisted, unable to face the thought of waiting alone, not knowing what was happening.

'It's bad enough having one irresponsible idiot up there without making it two.' His laugh was brief and harsh, the cutting edge searing Megan to the core.

'He's not an idiot,' flared Megan. 'He just wanted to go, and you stopped him,' she accused him, pointing an angry finger at him.

'Dead right I did,' he agreed readily. 'And with good

cause. And now we can see the results of his disobedience,' he reminded her firmly.

Megan hesitated for a moment while she thought about what he'd said, but she felt she had to defend Luke—he was only a child.

'If you'd let him go with the group this never would have happened,' she threw at him, delighted by the stunned expression on his face.

'So suddenly it's my fault?' he exclaimed, confronting her, expecting a sudden denial, but Megan was too angry now—angry and afraid.

'Yes. If you'd let him go with the group he'd be here now—safe,' she spat at him angrily. He was to blame. Her son was missing because of Darrow's stubbornness, his authoritarian attitude.

'He would be here and safe if he had done as he was told,' he said, with tight-lipped patience.

'He wanted to go to prove to you he could do it.' His unreasonable explanation of Luke's behaviour needed defending and she knew she was right. She could see the hero-worship Luke felt for Darrow even if Darrow couldn't.

'I see,' muttered Darrow, a cloud of understanding flickering in the deepest depths of his eyes. The colour drained from his face and he shut his eyes momentarily, as if to block out what Megan had said. His silence was unnerving, as if she had touched upon some raw, open wound, and the pain was so deep, so intense, that it robbed him of his ability to speak.

Suddenly his quietness was replaced by frustration and he burst out in agitation, 'Well, he's failed, hasn't he? All he has proved to me is that he can't be trusted.' He cursed under his breath as he pivoted away from her and marched for the door.

Megan was as quick on his heels as a new pup, and just as determined. She had never hated him so much as she did at that moment; where once she had loved him with a fierce intensity she now hated him with an equal amount of hate.

'You don't understand…' she shouted, stung by the sheer injustice of it all. If he knew Luke was his son he wouldn't be talking like this, she thought bitterly. But she had already decided she would not tell him, and somehow she felt he didn't even deserve to know—not now. He stopped suddenly, turning to face her, his eyes shining with unspent anger but his face a professional mask of composure.

'I do,' he snapped curtly. 'I understand perfectly. A child is missing, dusk is falling, and I'm wasting valuable time arguing with his mother, who seems determined to blame me for her own inadequacies.' His mouth clamped shut into a firm line, grim and uncompromising. His whole tone and attitude said that as far as he was concerned the conversation was over, and that any further discussion was totally pointless.

'*My* inadequacies?' breathed Megan in outrage.

'Yes, Megan. You failed to tell me Luke had been ill. Why? I'll tell you. Because you are obsessed with your image, and you wanted your son to match up, to be as strong and as healthy,' he snarled, sparing her none of his contempt. Megan stiffened, her body rigid with indignation. Though his assessment was uncannily accurate, it was simply none of his business.

'How dare you?' she exclaimed, the words rushing out in a heated flow, the hurt and pain of his criticism almost too much to bear under the circumstances.

'The truth hurts, doesn't it, Megan?' Darrow accused, sparing her nothing as his own temper grew. He raked his fingers through his thick mane of hair, his eyes skimming over her. 'Can't you see, Megan? Luke has not only put himself in danger but every one of the team who goes out to look for him.'

'You think I don't know that?' cried Megan, distraught, her voice beginning to break with the strain as the initial shock wore off, to be replaced by a terrible sense of dread. The stiffness left Darrow's jaw, the thin line of his mouth softening as his mouth curved briefly into a half-smile. He rested his hand softly on Megan's shoulder.

'He'll be all right,' he reassured her, but Megan pulled away, no longer able to bear his touch. All her emotions were trained on one person, and that was her son, lost out on the barren hills.

Megan glanced again at her watch. The minutes seemed to be passing so slowly, and with each second her hope died a little more. She ranged round the room, unable to settle, periodically going to the window to scan the deserted road. The night was falling fast and the air was definitely cooling. She cast another nervous glance at the clock as her stomach twisted yet again. She lifted a cup to her mouth, but the once hot coffee was now cold and she gave a grimace of distance as she put it back down. She didn't really want a drink anyway; it was just something to do, she thought miserably, returning to the window.

She gave a silent gasp as the flash of headlights illuminated the dark road and she flew to the door, yanking it back and rushing out just as the Jeep drew to a halt. Darrow was climbing out of the rear door, Luke held securely in his arms.

'Go back in the house.' He barked the order at Megan,

indifferent to the trauma she was going through. She stormed back inside, her heart thudding with a mixture of outrage and fear. In that quick glance she had noticed that there was no movement from Luke, and she couldn't help but wonder if Darrow was protecting her from some awful truth.

'Get a bowl of hot water and some antiseptic.' Darrow's sharp voice shattered her thoughts as he entered, carrying her child with amazing ease and resting him gently down on to the large leather couch. Darrow sank beside him, his face taut, his features still bearing the strain.

'Come on, Megan,' he called, so his voice would carry to the kitchen where she was fetching cotton wool, water and antiseptic. She returned instantly, her face troubled, and took a quick glance at her son, her frown deepening. 'He'll come round in a bit,' he told her, taking the first-aid items from her before barking yet another order. 'Make up a cold compress. He took quite a tumble and there's going to be a real bump on his head.'

'It's quite all right,' snapped Megan as she saw Luke begin to stir, her relief flooding her with sudden confidence and outrage at his interference. 'I can manage now,' she finished sharply, wanting him to move so that she could sit at the side of her son, see to his needs.

Darrow breathed in deeply, his eyes flashing to hers in annoyance. 'I've no intention of going anywhere,' he snapped. 'I'm staying here till I am satisfied that Luke is all right, so you might as well get used to the idea,' he explained in a tone that brooked no argument. Megan might have said more, but at that moment Luke groaned loudly, his eyes flickering open.

'Mum—Mum?' he asked, turning his head slightly to see her, any pretence of maturity forgotten. He was like a little child, looking for the reassurance of his mother. Megan sank to her knees, her eyes misting over with unshed tears, and she took his hand, squeezing it gently.

'I'm here, Luke,' she said softly. 'You're home now,' she assured him as she stroked his hair from his forehead.

'How are you, Luke?' asked Darrow, his voice clear but edged with a hardness that Megan instinctively noticed.

'OK, I think. My head aches,' he answered, rubbing his hands lightly over his forehead with a frown.

'It will do,' Darrow informed him coldly, and the puzzled frown of pain cleared immediately from Luke's face, to be replaced by one of dislike. 'You've been lucky—very lucky. You had a short fall, resulting in only a few cuts and bruises,' he told him as he began to wring the warm water from the cotton wool.

'What do you think you're doing?' snapped Luke as he eyed Darrow warily, moving as far away as he could on the couch.

'I'm going to clean up these cuts while you're mother makes something to eat,' he informed him, casting a glance at Megan to gauge her reaction. She flushed, the resentment glittering in her eyes matching Luke's perfectly, but neither of them made any objections.

'Keep still,' Darrow ordered as Luke tried to twist away. 'These wounds are quite dirty, and if they're not properly cleaned they could easily become infected,' he warned.

'I can do it myself,' complained Luke with a scowl.

'Can you? Well, I've the privilege so keep still,' he returned coolly as he began to dab away at the dry encrusted blood and dirt that surrounded a gash on his right arm. The moment the sharp sting of the antiseptic touched the exposed area Luke winced, taking a deep breath.

'I thought you were going to make something to eat,' barked Darrow, turning to glare at Megan, who was grimacing each time he touched Luke. She glared back at him and reluctantly climbed to her feet.

'What do you want, Luke?' she asked, effectively blocking out Darrow as she purposely concentrated on her son.

'Something light but wholesome,' cut in Darrow. 'Chicken soup,' he ordered smoothly, returning his attention back to the work in hand.

Luke remained silent, watching Darrow's every move with caution, so Megan turned on her heel and marched into the kitchen, slamming open doors and crashing pots and pans to relieve some of the build-up of frustration she was feeling. Darrow raised his eyebrows in mock-horror in Luke's direction, and they shared a conspiratorial grin.

'Can you manage to take off these jeans?' Darrow asked, eyeing the torn jeans dubiously. It was obvious that they were hiding yet another abrasion; they were stained with the dark red hue of old blood. Luke nodded and struggled to his feet, leaning on Darrow for support as he hopped out of his jeans and sank quickly back on the couch, closing his eyes, exhausted by the effort.

'It's not as bad as I thought,' murmured Darrow, examining the wound with an expert eye. 'It certainly doesn't need stitching, but I think it would be as well to keep it covered for a few days,' he informed him, but received no reply. Luke was too tired even to answer. Darrow carefully inspected every cut, pleased that they were all minor.

'Have you any aspirin?' Darrow asked as Megan came

back into the room, carrying a tray holding a bowl of steaming soup and a crusty bread roll. She nodded as she passed him the tray.

'For you or Luke?' she asked.

'Both of us,' he admitted with a wry smile, and Megan felt a stab of guilt. It was only in that moment that she saw just how weary he looked, and how much the night's events had taken out of him. His eyes were surrounded by dark shadows and his hair was in disarray, only seeming to emphasise the tiredness that clung to his rugged features, making them look drawn and tired.

'I won't be a minute.' She smiled. 'Do you want some soup?' she added, not knowing whether she wanted him to accept her offer or not, but deciding not to dwell on it too much. Besides, it was the least she could do.

By the time she returned Luke was tucking into his soup. He still looked tired and a little pale, but other than that he was fine, she could tell. Darrow accepted his bowl of soup, sipping it with a nod of appreciation, and as Luke finished Megan darted up, taking away the tray.

'I think it would be best if you went to bed now, Luke,' she told him briskly, offering him the aspirin and a glass of milk. He threw his head back as he swallowed the tablets and grimaced as a pain shot through his head. He tried to get to his feet, too tired even to argue, but his limbs were awkward and beginning to stiffen up.

'I'll help you,' Darrow offered, putting his food to one side, but Luke flashed him a look of anger.

'I'll be OK,' he muttered as he struggled to his feet.

'I said I'll help you, and it's about time you realised you can't always do what you want,' he snapped, getting to his feet and clasping Luke around the waist. Fiercely independent, Luke tried to shrug away, but it was a futile gesture. 'God, but you're stubborn!' exclaimed Darrow in exasperation.

'I wonder where he gets that from?' said Megan, forgetting herself in defence of her own son. She flushed immediately once the words were spoken, and she lowered her lashes over her eyes, to hide the guilt she knew would shine there.

'His mother,' grinned Darrow, convinced that she was making a joke at her own expense.

Megan tried to smile in return, but somehow the relief was mixed with hurt that he had not seen the truth.

'Come on, Luke, rest your weight on me,' he instructed as he steered him towards the door. Megan remained staring after them, lost in her own thoughts, until Darrow suddenly reappeared, raking his thick hair from his face, revealing the exhaustion that was etched so clearly on his drawn features.

'He's more tired than anything else—emotionally and physically drained,' he informed her, and the description could have fitted him equally well, thought Megan, suddenly moved by compassion. After all, she felt responsible—it was her son's fault really.

'Would you like a coffee?' she offered, moving towards the kitchen. 'Help yourself to a brandy—you look as if you need it,' she added, inclining her head towards the corner table, where sat a number of bottles.

'Do you want one?' he asked as he poured himself a generous measure into a crystal brandy glass, swirling the amber liquid round in its balloon shape in appreciation.

'Yes, thanks,' agreed Megan, placing two cups of coffee down on the table and moving over to turn on the fire. The sudden blaze of heat took the chill from the room and she curled up on the floor near the fire, watching the flickering flames dance between the black coals. Darrow sat down in a chair, his eyes closing slightly as he sipped the brandy. Megan cast him a covert glance from under her hooded lids.

'I'm sorry about all this, Darrow, and about the things I said—' she began as she cupped her coffee-cup tightly in her hands, trying to lose her self-consciousness in the black liquid.

'It's me who owes you an apology,' he cut in sharply. 'I was way out of line a couple of times,' he said coolly, his eyes opening and resting on her for a moment, trying to gauge her response to him.

'It's quite all right. I understand,' Megan said swiftly. She didn't want this. She could cope so much better when they were at loggerheads rather than on this dangerously friendly level. Any hopes she'd had of a reconciliation between them had vanished when she'd seen the antipathy between Luke and Darrow. It was obvious they would never be friends.

'No, I said a lot of things I had no right to.' His eyes flared with the sudden light of anger, directed more at himself than her. 'I was angry, but that was no excuse for blaming you. If anyone was at fault, it was me. I should have anticipated what Luke's response would be, but I was too preoccupied with us to think straight,' he admitted in a grim tone.

'It's all right,' Megan said again, this time with genuine understanding, and she took a mouthful of her brandy, enjoying the flare of heat it gave to her body.

'I also think you were probably right,' he continued, refusing to let the subject drop. 'Luke was trying to impress me. I realised that when we found him. His major concern was how I felt about him.'

'And you told him?' asked Megan, hating the thought

of Darrow venting his anger on her son, whether he deserved it or not.

'No,' he answered sharply. 'Not yet. But I intend to
speak to him about it,' he added grimly, and Megan knew
there was nothing she could do or say that would stop
him. She rose to her feet to replenish her coffee, her hand
trembling slightly as she poured. She could feel Darrow's
heated, hungry gaze on her, and found it unnerving.

'Do you want another?' she asked, praying that he
would refuse. But he didn't. He shrugged instead as he
passed her his cup. She caught the gleam of brittle impatience in his eyes and knew that this polite conversation was annoying him.

'Megan, we have to talk—sort something out,' he said,
putting his cup down and reaching out to remove hers
from her hand. He wanted no barriers between them.

'There's nothing to sort out, Darrow,' she muttered.
There might once have been a chance, but not now. The
chasm between Luke and Darrow was unbridgeable.
They would never be friends; there was too much antag-
onism between them—a rivalry that would only increase
if she was foolish enough to become involved with
Darrow again.

A tight, angry frown knitted his brow as he caught hold
of her wrist, the sudden action sending shock-waves
through her body. She had almost forgotten how potent
his touch could be. She tried to move away but he rose,
drawing her even closer to him.

'We have to try, Megan,' he said huskily, his warm
breath heating her face, deepening the pink flush that had
so easily risen to her cheeks. She tried to pull away, but
her own resistance was low.

'Leave me alone,' she said, forcing her voice to be

strong. She couldn't let him know, let him see how much she loved him.

'No—no, I won't,' he said emphatically. 'We could have a future together.' He moved even closer, till his body was against hers. He was aware of the weakening effect that would have, and Megan stiffened as his thigh brushed against hers. She ignored the hope and desire in his voice, refusing to respond to it.

'No, there can be no future between us,' she told him, her heart tearing in two with every word, but she had no choices left. Part of her longed to have Darrow in her life, but not at Luke's expense. He dropped his hands on to her shoulders, clamping his fingers around them as his gaze searched her face.

'You're hurting me,' she breathed as his fingers sank into her skin, and she watched him close his eyes to block out her words. The pressure of his fingers relaxed a little, but she was still trapped by him, longing for an escape she knew wouldn't come.

'I'm sorry,' he muttered, sighing as he spoke. 'You hurt me too,' he said softly, offering it as an explanation.

His hand began a soft descent over her back, as if to massage all the hurt away. Megan felt herself move to the security of his powerful chest as her knees seemed to give way. Her heartbeat was raging so fast that it frightened her. She felt his arms wrap around her waist, drawing her closer to him, and with familiar ease she raised her face to allow him to capture her willing lips. The kiss was sweet and gentle, yet there as an undercurrent of power that she responded to. The flames of desire spiralled through her body, drawing them even closer together.

He awoke in her all the passion that had lain dormant for so long. The hunger and need threatened to overwhelm her, but she could not allow herself such an indulgence. He wanted her, she knew that, but he had wanted her before, had promised to be faithful then had left her for someone else. Besides, there was Luke to consider.

These thoughts had an instantly sobering effect. She pushed the palms of her hands hard on to his chest, forcing him from her.

'No, Darrow,' she said firmly, trying to ignore the heated passion that shone from his gleaming eyes.

'No?' he queried, a lazy smile curling his lips in disbelief, his arms returning to encircle her waist. 'I know you want to, Meggie,' he drawled confidently, pulling her softly towards him again. 'It's just like old times, only better.' His voice was smoky, almost hypnotic.

'It's in the past. Like you said, old times,' she spat at him bitterly, trying to hide her pain as she pulled herself free. He did not move after her but stood staring at her, his breathing ragged with desire and the glitter of angry frustration flaring in the depths of his eyes. Megan pushed her tousled hair from her face, her action betraying her nervousness as she watched him closely.

He was close to the edge, his features taking on a hardened savagery and his volatile temper bubbling close to the surface, though he was keeping a tight rein on it, and the strain was visible in the tension in his jaw. For a moment they just stared at each other, unable to speak, till the silence was broken by a faint call.

'Mum! Mum!'

Megan turned immediately, making her way to the stairs, so grateful for the interruption. But she stopped, frozen on the middle stair, when she heard the slam of the door. It reverberated through the house, as if mocking her and emphasising her empty life. Megan had never felt so lonely in all her life, and a chill stole across her heart.

It took longer than she thought to settle Luke; he still needed a lot of reassurance, and she sat with him, talking quietly to him till he went back to sleep.

Finally she went back downstairs to lock up. She half-heartedly picked up the cups and glasses, placing them on the draining-board. There was something sadly poignant about the two glasses and two cups, and despite herself she looked across at the hotel room she knew to be Darrow's. His light was still on and it gave her a grim satisfaction to know that he was finding it as difficult as she was to relax.

It was poor consolation that she had made her decision in order to protect Luke, but she knew it was the right one—the only one, she repeated to herself. Even if she had fallen in love with Darrow again nothing could come of it, and hot, salty tears splashed down her face in silent rivers.

CHAPTER EIGHT

MEGAN spent the next few days at her mother's house, safely away from Darrow. She was surprised when the letter arrived for her.

Her fingers trembled slightly, her eyes quickly scanning the letter again in order to convince herself of its authenticity. She sank on to her mother's battered old rocking-chair and read the letter again. It was so unbelievable, and her emotions were so confused. After all these years she had a father—a father who wanted to meet her.

Megan went straight to the hotel to book a table for her and her father; she felt a relaxing dinner was the ideal opportunity to meet.

'A table for two,' she requested, her voice almost a whisper with excitement.

'Two?' A sharp voice queried behind her, making her jump. She spun round to face a grim-looking Darrow.

'Oh, Darrow,' she gasped in surprise.

'Two?' he queried again. His voice sounded strained and a frown scurried across his brow.

'A friend,' Megan said evasively—she didn't want to share her secret with anyone.

'Someone important?' he asked, obviously intrigued by the excitement that she was trying desperately to bank down.

'Very,' she answered, trying to move away, but Darrow was determined to know more.

'An old school friend? Joanne Power?' he encouraged.

'No, he's not an old school friend,' Megan admitted.

'A he?' Darrow's voice sounded more serious now, and for a fleeting moment Megan wondered whether or not he was jealous. She guessed not.

'He must be keen to see you if he has followed you on your holiday—two weeks' separation too long?' he commented, his voice sharp with disapproval, but Megan was oblivious to his feelings, too preoccupied with her own joy.

'I can't wait to see him,' she agreed, strolling away, her whole body alive with joy.

Megan wasted no time. Within moments she had made all the arrangements, and by tomorrow evening she would be meeting her father—a meeting that she was really looking forward to but at the same time dreading.

Luke had received the news with a coolness that she'd found irksome, but nothing could dampen the excitement that was twirling through her body, making her heart race in anticipation. Luke declined her offer of joining them for dinner, assuring Megan that the first time it should be just the two of them alone. He would be all right, he insisted, and she was secretly glad.

She wanted to meet her father alone, to see and talk with him before she had to share him with anyone else. There was so much she wanted to know, and her feelings towards him were so confused. Why had he sent the letter? How long ago? Had he really loved her mother? Why hadn't he married her—been a proper father to Megan? She wasn't even sure she'd like him—the odds against it seemed to be stacked impossibly high—and yet some deep, dark part of her soul already felt a bond.

Luke watched Megan pace nervously up and down the room the next evening with a bemused look on his face.

'You're going to wear a path in that carpet,' he commented drily as he watched her actions with interest.

'I can't help it—I'm a nervous wreck,' Megan admitted, the butterflies in her stomach taking flight yet again.

'At least you have a father,' Luke said softly, with all the longing that Megan herself had felt so often. She turned swiftly to face him, stopping immediately as she saw the pain in his eyes. A pink tinge of guilt coloured her cheeks and she clasped him tightly to her.

'Oh, Luke, I'm so sorry,' she gasped, hugging him slightly.

'It's hardly your fault my father died,' he said, forcing a smile as he pulled away, embarrassed by this show of emotion. Megan released him as the doorbell rang, but her eyes followed him. Should she tell him? How would he react? It was all so difficult.

'I'm off now,' Luke called, and Megan hurried to the door to see who he was going with. She stopped in her tracks, stunned by Luke's companion.

'Good evening, Megan,' Darrow drawled, a smile of triumph curling his lips and the light of interest in his lambent eyes as he made a quick appraisal of her. Megan frowned as she shifted uncomfortably under his cool scrutiny. 'Meeting that someone special?' he asked. It was obvious that she had made a great effort with her appearance. Her make-up was perfect, her jade-green silk dress emphasised her marvellous red hair and reflected her cool, molten green eyes.

'Yes,' she answered stiffly, her mouth a thin line of disapproval as she flashed a look at Luke. 'I didn't know you were going out with Darrow,' she said, her disappointment edged with anger as it only served to increase her feelings of guilt and worry.

'You didn't ask. Why, have you a problem with that?' challenged Luke, putting Megan deliberately on the spot.

'No. No, not at all; why should I?' she said airily, hiding her true feelings behind the mask of a smile. 'Where are you going?' she asked, intrigued, her gaze returning to Darrow who was watching her with an intensity she felt strangely excited by.

'Pizzeria in the town centre,' Darrow told her coolly. 'Ready?' he asked, turning his attention back to Luke, who nodded readily in agreement. 'I'll bring him back safely,' Darrow informed Megan, a hint of mockery in his cool tone, and he flashed her a grin that showed his predatory teeth. Megan wondered what he was up to, though she feigned indifference.

'I'm sure you will,' she said with a stiff smile as she watched them walk down the drive, already deep in conversation. It seemed so odd. Why on earth should Luke and Darrow go out for a meal? She hadn't realised their relationship had changed so dramatically. It might be innocent enough, she mused, but she could not shake off the niggling doubts that stirred restlessly through her mind. The last thing she needed was for Luke to forge a relationship with Darrow—it would only complicate things even more.

She glanced at her watch. Ten to eight—time to go. She had booked a table in the hotel restaurant for eight.

She walked into the hotel foyer, her quick strides betraying her nervousness. She faltered slightly as she saw him. She knew he was her father; some natural instinct seemed to wake in her, and she stared at him as spontaneous tears welled in her eyes. The depth of emotion that this stranger aroused in her was bewildering, and she could tell she was having an equal impact on him, though neither of them had spoken.

'Hello, I'm Megan,' she finally said, her voice almost breaking with the powerful feelings that were surging through her body.

'Megan,' he repeated, as if murmuring some dark secret from his past. 'Megan, darling.'

They moved in unison, directed by some unseen force, their arms opening to hug each other, and the dam against the tears broke as they both sobbed.

It took some time before they were calm enough to go into dinner, but all doubts that the evening would be an ordeal had now vanished.

'Please—please sit down,' Megan told him with a smile as she searched his face for some common likeness.

'Yes,' he agreed readily, drawing out Megan's chair first, like an old-fashioned gentleman. 'We have so much to discuss,' he said, his eyes as bright as buttons as he watched her, memories of her mother rushing to greet him.

'I can't believe this,' admitted Megan, a little breathless, her eyes never leaving his face. She wanted to absorb it, catch each detail and store it for future memory.

'You're very much like your mother,' he told her, his smile soft and warm with love. 'I'm sorry about her death; I should have liked to see her again,' he said wistfully as he rested his hand over Megan's, and she rejoiced at the feel of it.

'Tell me what happened. When did you first know about me?' she asked, convinced that he must only recently have found out about her. He hesitated for a moment, as if he realised his answer would come as a disappointment.

'Your mother told me in the first month of her pregnancy,' he confessed quietly, hating the sharp light of pain that lit Megan's eyes.

'What?' she asked in disbelief, anger replacing her pain. Her mother had never seemed doomed, as if she had been rejected by the man she loved.

'I wanted to marry her, Megan, believe me,' he said, squeezing her hand in reassurance, just as she had imagined fathers would do, but now the gesture seemed a futile waste. 'Nothing would have given me greater pleasure—' he continued, but Megan cut in, refusing to be carried away by emotion.

'So why didn't you?' she demanded. 'Were you already married?' she asked, toying with her napkin in agitation with her free hand.

'No, not then,' he sighed, knowing that it would be difficult to explain. 'Your mother didn't want to marry me. She quite simply wanted a child, not a husband,' he said, with a sad simplicity that melted Megan's heart. With understanding she nodded in acceptance of his explanation.

'She was a very independent lady,' Megan said in agreement. She had never really understood her mother, and this only confirmed just how different they had been. 'So how did you find me?' she asked, intrigued.

They paused for a moment, hating the intrusion, but the waiter wanted their order.

'I don't even know what you like,' he laughed, listening attentively to her choice and nodding that he would have the same. It seemed to act as a sealing bond.

'I never would have found you, but your mother changed her mind. I don't know why—she always said that I should never see you, that you were to be her child and hers alone, so I was completely taken by surprise when I received a letter from her. She had given it to her solicitor to be passed on to me in the event of her death.

It has naturally taken some time to find me. I've changed addresses several times, as you can imagine.'

'I wonder what changed her mind?' mused Megan. It was so unlike her mother—she had been very determined, and once her mind had been made up no one could change it.

'The letter was about thirteen years old,' he said, as if trying to remember. 'So maybe something happened to change her mind,' he said thoughtfully. Megan guessed the reason, and it wasn't a 'what', it was a 'who'—Luke.

'I think I know. Not only have you a daughter, but also a grandson,' Megan said, and was delighted by his reaction.

'A grandson?' he echoed. 'But where? How old is he, and why did that make any difference to your mother?'

'It's a long story,' began Megan, suddenly glad that she had someone to confide in, and she began to spill out her past, adding the recent events to clarify matters. He nodded as she spoke, neither congratulating her nor condemning her, which made her confession so much easier. Time seemed to whiz by, and by their fourth cup of coffee the staff were beginning to fidget.

'I think it's time we went,' Megan grinned, getting to her feet with reluctance.

'I guess so,' he agreed a little sorrowfully, and they made their way to the foot of the stairs.

'I have to go back tomorrow,' he began, with deep regret in his voice, his eyes misting over as he looked at her. 'But now I've found you...' His voice trailed away as the emotion became too strong. Megan came quickly to his rescue.

'Are you sure you're ready for parenthood?' she laughed, trying to inject some lightness back into the evening.

'Remember you have two half-brothers and a half-sister to meet yet.' He smiled as he reached out to stroke her hair, the gesture forcing Megan to swallow the painful lump in her throat.

'I can't wait to meet them,' she said quietly, already dreading the moment of parting. 'And there's your grandson, remember.'

'Talking of Luke,' he said seriously, his eyes fixed firmly on her, 'I know how it feels to be robbed of a child. Tell Darrow. He deserves to know, and so does Luke.'

Megan opened her mouth to protest, but he shook his head. 'Tell them, Megan. Regardless of what has happened between you and Darrow, you have no right to keep them apart.'

'I know,' she confessed quietly, understanding the terrible mistake she had made and determined to make amends despite the consequences.

'Good girl, and I'll see you soon,' he said, his words filling her with joy.

'Yes, yes.' She smiled back, flinging her arms about him in one last embrace, and they held each other as if they never wanted to let go.

'Goodnight, Megan,' he whispered. 'Let's say goodbye now. I'm leaving early in the morning and I don't think I could go through this again.'

'Yes, I know,' sobbed Megan, squeezing him yet again, so tightly that he gasped. How could she deny Luke this? she thought as she drew back, accepting the proffered handkerchief and dabbing her eyes. 'Goodbye...' She faltered, then added with a smile, 'Goodbye, Daddy,' and he grinned in response.

'Goodnight and God bless, daughter.' Then he turned and began to climb the stairs, pausing at the top for one

final wave. Megan waved back as the tears fell, blinding
her eyes and preventing her from seeing Darrow's arrival.
He frowned at the sight of her tears and took a quick
glance up the stairs, curious to know who the older man
was that he had just seen. Luke's passing remark that she
was meeting a man who meant more to her than anybody
had both angered and intrigued him. He had to know who
he was, but Luke had been so evasive, refusing to divulge
who the mystery man was.

'You OK, Megan?' he asked sharply. 'It's getting late
and I was wondering what had happened to you.' There
was censure in his tone and that irked her.

'Yes, I'm all right. Did you have a good time?' she
asked, not wishing to discuss her father with him, nor
with anyone. She wanted him all to herself for as long
as possible. She had sworn Luke to secrecy. She had
waited so long for him that she was not prepared to share
him yet.

'Luke is good company. I enjoyed myself—and you?
Luke told me it was a very special occasion for you,' he
said a little pointedly, his eyes darkening as he viewed
her. He didn't wait for a reply but continued. 'I should
have thought he was a little old for you,' he commented
drily.

'He's old enough to be my father,' snapped back Megan, angered by his interruption; it somehow sullied her
evening. She pivoted away from him, eager to be away,
but Darrow moved quicker, pulling her back, his face a
hard, granite mask, his expression a confused mixture of
anger and desire.

'What's wrong with you, Megan?' he bit out at her,
his teeth clenched. 'Why are you always running away
from me?' he taunted, drawing her close and silencing
her protestations by covering her lips with his.

The kiss was deep and passionate, revealing a hunger that was desperate for satisfaction as they both responded, losing themselves in a breathless sea of desire. Suddenly Megan felt herself pushed away, held at arm's length. Her eyes shot open and she was confronted with a look of bitter triumph on Darrow's ruthless face.

'Does he make you feel like that, Megan? I doubt it. Deny it all you want, Meggie, but I know you come alive in my arms,' he taunted, before turning away and leaving her alone, stunned and so very angry.

Megan stormed home, slamming the door to release some of her temper before marching into the lounge. Luckily Luke had already gone to bed—she could hear the faint sound of his radio from his bedroom—and she sat down, her mind in a turmoil. This had been one of the most perfect nights of her life and it had been ruined by—by—by that—

'Pig!' she exclaimed loudly.

He didn't deserve to know about Luke. It was all very well her father saying he had the right to know, and before she had been so sure, but not now. At least her father had wanted to marry her mother. He hadn't rejected her, fallen in love with someone else in a matter of months, deserting her completely to struggle alone. But Darrow had. Darrow was guilty while her father was innocent. Her father deserved a chance, but Darrow... She mused till her head ached.

Then there was Luke. How would he react? Would he turn against her, reject her as his father had done, and was she prepared to take that risk?

She was so confused that any chance of sleep had evaporated. She felt awake, alert, her mind buzzing, so she decided to sit out on the balcony. There was a full moon hanging in the clear sky and the night air was crisp and invigorating. She settled herself down on a patio chair, wrapping her coat firmly around her shoulders as she gazed out into the blackness of the night.

The moon illuminated the lake, sending a steam of silvery light across the water, and she watched it, mesmerised, till she caught a sudden movement. Her eyes scanned the deserted road. She was sure she had seen someone, but despite straining her eyes she could see nothing. The cries of the night animals filled the air, making it all seem sinister, and she gave an involuntary shiver.

Then she saw him again, just beyond the road, making his way to the shore of the lake. Megan stood up, leaning out to have a better view as the light of the moon caught his face. It was Darrow.

Megan watched with interest as he idly began to pick up pebbles from the shore and skim them across the water. It was a familiar childhood game called ducks and drakes. He had always been the more skilful player—sometimes he had been able to make just one pebble hit the water fifteen times before it sank into oblivion. Tonight he was not as lucky—maybe it was his choice of stone, she mused idly as she watched him, intrigued by his actions. It was fun watching him from a safe distance, and yet part of her longed to join him, for him to want to take her by the hand, so that they could walk hand in hand along the shore with the moon as their only light.

It was a romantic dream that could never come true. She knew she must tell him about Luke, but knew that once she had it would never be the same between them. She could never forgive him for what he had done to her, and she knew that she would never fully trust him again. She still loved him; she had never stopped—which was probably why all her other attempts at relationships had failed. She'd never wanted to become seriously involved with anyone; it hadn't seemed fair to them when she really loved someone else.

The decision to tell him made Megan suddenly feel that there was a load off her mind, and she closed the door, casting one last look at Darrow before going to bed.

Megan slept surprisingly well. She woke up refreshed and clear-headed. She hadn't felt so positive in a long time. First she would tell Darrow, then they could face Luke together with the news. She was not looking forward to either interview but somehow there was a sense of relief, of shaking off a burden she had been carrying alone for so long.

She showered, massaging her skin afterwards with a blend of almond oil and marigold cream. She blow-dried her hair into a neat bob and chose a simple but well-cut navy dress to wear. She checked her face in her compact then slipped it into her shoulder-bag, pulling the bag up so that it rested neatly at her side. Luke was still in bed as she made her way to the hotel, determined to see Darrow first thing.

The receptionist rang through to his office and Darrow came out to greet her. He was dressed very formally, which initially took her by surprise because she remembered that there was a barbecue arranged for later today. He was wearing a simple, plain navy suit, a crisp white shirt that had a thin navy line running through it, and a sombre-looking tie. He suddenly looked older and serious, and Megan's courage almost failed her. He had a sheaf of papers in his hand and a distracted frown furrowed his brow. He raked his fingers through his hair as he turned to the receptionist.

'Are we still using the McFergusons for the cheeses?'

he asked, ignoring Megan for a moment as he waited for a reply.

'Of course. Is there any reason why we shouldn't?' the woman retorted, a little briskly, as if she was fed up with his constant questions.

'No, it just appears that there's a discrepancy in this account. I just wanted it clarified.' His tone was equally curt, and Megan flinched at the sharp look that accompanied his words, though the receptionist seemed impervious to his glaring eyes. 'If you'd like to come through,' he said to Megan coolly as he turned back into his office, and she followed him, her heart sinking. Once the door was closed he put down the papers and raised his eyes to look at her.

'Her boyfriend works for the McFerguson company, and I'm sure there's something going on,' he said grimly as his eyes skimmed the columns again, unable to make sense of the accounts.

'Numbers were never your strong point.' Megan laughed at the memory. He had always been a writer, had a natural gift for words, but numbers were totally incomprehensible to him. 'Can I see?' she asked. It was like old times—she had often helped him with his maths while he was at school.

'Gladly,' he said, expelling a huge sigh of relief as he passed over the papers. 'Coffee?' he offered, pouring some dark, strong-smelling coffee into a mug.

'Have you milk?' she asked, remembering his habit of drinking black coffee—a throw-back to his student days, when he had always been running out of milk.

'Yes,' he said, waving a tiny catering tub at her with a smile that creased his face. 'And sugar,' he added, waving a tiny sachet at her incredulous face.

'Good, I'll have both,' she said with a nod. 'It looks

as though I'll need it.' She glanced back at the papers. 'Is this your handiwork?' she asked with a grimace.

'You can tell,' he said in mock-disappointment, passing her a coffee and perching on the edge of the desk next to her.

'Instantly recognisable,' she mocked, and his smile widened till creases ran down either side of his face.

'Do you remember Mrs Marne? She hated me,' Darrow said with a grin.

'The feeling was mutual. You drove that poor teacher to despair,' recalled Megan.

'I just couldn't grasp maths,' he confessed a little sheepishly.

'No, you couldn't,' she agreed. 'Whereas I had a natural aptitude for figures and more patience than Mrs Marne.'

'You helped me a great deal,' he said with affection, looking at her closely as the years seemed to fall away.

'It was the least I could do. You saved me from all that bullying and name-calling,' she reminded him, quite unnecessarily.

'It was my pleasure,' he said graciously.

'Not always. You fought many a fist-fight on my account,' she said, hating the painful scenes that rushed through her mind.

'It was a good job I was big for my age,' he admitted ruefully, taking a mouthful of coffee.

'It certainly helped,' agreed Megan, quickly fixing her attention on the papers. This kind of conversation was dangerously intimate. It stirred in them both feelings that were best left dormant.

'How did last night go?' he said, suddenly serious, his smile fading slightly as he spoke, and Megan was immediately alert. She cocked her head to one side, looking at him quizzically.

'Fine,' she said simply, but her heart was beating out a rapid tattoo as she wondered how much she should tell Darrow.

'I owe you another apology. I seem to be doing a lot of that lately,' he admitted, his tone full of remorse. 'God, I don't know why I behave like that,' he said in sudden frustration, pushing himself away from the desk. Megan watched his action, knowing he was fighting an inner battle. He was attracted to her, wanted her, was even jealous—but love had never entered his mind, it was so alien to him.

'Forget it and find me last year's accounts,' she said efficiently, pushing the fact that he didn't love her to the back of her mind as she tried to convince herself that it didn't matter.

'Can you get them yourself? They're over there in the cabinet.' He cast a quick glance at his watch. 'Look, I'm late for an appointment with the bank—can you cope?' he asked hopefully.

'Naturally,' Megan grinned. She was used to working and with Luke occupied time had hung heavily on her hands. This work was a welcome distraction.

'What did you come to see me for?' he asked as he opened the door to leave.

'I'll tell you later.'

'OK—and thanks for your help. We always did make a great team,' he added, unaware of the pride she felt at his words. He closed the door behind him and Megan immediately went to the cabinet to look for the files she needed.

She began to rummage through. Finding them proved no problem, but Megan couldn't close the cabinet shut.

She pushed against it with all her might, but to no avail. Something was jamming the back of it. She reached into the furthest corner of the cabinet, her fingers feeling a large package. It was stuck fast, but with careful man-oeuvring she retrieved a large manila envelope. She wiped the dark dust form the edges and looked at the writing scrawled across the front.

Broken Promises.

She tore the envelope open and pulled out the manu-script for a book. She read the opening line and gave a gasp of dismay.

Carrie was beautiful, the perfect example of a Californian beach baby. She had long blonde hair and even longer, suntanned legs. She was the image of my American dream-girl. Her eyes were as blue as the Pacific Ocean, where I spent most of my time that first summer in the States.

Megan couldn't help it. She wanted to read on, but she dared not take the risk of being found, so she quickly pushed the envelope deep into her bag, pulling the zip across to conceal the contents.

She was even more determined to finish the accounts now, and worked at fever-pitch, soon finding that there *had* been some tampering with the stock, a fact that she would point out to Darrow later. She quickly pushed all her work back into the file, then carefully put it back in the cabinet. Then, swinging her bag over her shoulder, she went back home, eager to read the manuscript.

It was the best thing Darrow had ever written. It was warm, compassionate, sometimes exciting, then it all started to go terribly wrong.

Carrie left the hero for someone else, leaving him unable to cope. Megan could tell how much Carrie had meant to Darrow—the feelings of love the hero had for her were certainly written from the heart, and the sense of desolation when she married was beautifully written. Megan's heart went out to Darrow; she felt sure the story was true. It was so accurate—it described how she had felt when Darrow had left her so perfectly. She couldn't put it down, and two hours later she was wiping a tear from her face. She knew it was good—very good— though she wondered if she identified with it too closely.

She now knew why Darrow had come back—there had been nothing left for him in America. That hurt, though why she didn't know. What had she expected? His return to have something to do with her? Impossible—all his emotions had been spent on Carrie. Yet she couldn't let her own disappointment prevent his writing career.

Quickly she flipped through her address book, then tapped out a number in a rapid tattoo. Her friend Sue had been in publishing for years and could spot a bestseller at a hundred yards, and Megan was quite convinced that this story had all the required elements. She was desperate for a second opinion.

An hour later she handed over a neatly parcelled manuscript to Mrs Bain, who noted the publisher's address with interest but made no comment. Megan glanced at her watch. Time had flown by and she had promised Luke that she would be at the barbecue. She was going to be late, she thought with a frown as she began the long walk back to the hotel.

She hoped Darrow wouldn't notice the missing manuscript. It didn't seem likely, by its battered condition.

Megan guessed it had been placed there and forgotten a long time ago—but what would she say if he did miss it? she thought, suddenly worried.

I'll just have to bluff my way out of it, she decided, increasing the pace of her steps with determination.

CHAPTER NINE

MEGAN was quickly out of her formal dress and into a pair of snug-fitting jeans and a white bodysuit. She pulled a pair of chunky white trainers onto her feet, grabbed her keys, and made her way to the barbecue. The smell of burning pine-wood scented the air, mingling with the enticing aromas of outdoor cooking, and Megan suddenly felt hungry.

It was quite a large gathering. Children played noisily, supervised by one of the helpers, while the older youngsters had gravitated towards the music, lounging on the grass as they listened to the noisy sounds that vibrated through the air.

Megan scanned the group for Luke. She couldn't see him but she was forced to admit that food would be his major interest. Several large buffet tables were groaning with food—there was a huge array of salads, dishes of relish, and a mountain of baked potatoes and sweetcorn cobs, dripping with melted golden butter.

Megan had guessed right. Luke with amazing dexterity, was balancing an overflowing plate in one hand and a large tumbler of Coke in the other. She couldn't see who he was talking to at first—too many people blocked her view—but she stopped in mid-track when she did see who it was. Darrow. They were both laughing uproariously at some shared joke. Their closeness was undeniable, and Megan drew nearer cautiously, her ears straining to hear the conversation.

'I'm not sure,' Luke was saying thoughtfully. 'I've

thought of journalism, but I like the idea of doing something for the environment.'

'You could combine the two,' replied Darrow, a smile almost of indulgence curling his mouth, which took Megan by complete surprise.

'I guess so.' Luke shrugged expressively before adding, 'I have to take my exams first.'

'I think the timetable we worked out will enable you to retain the right balance between work and play,' said Darrow, watching Luke's eating habits with a faint trace of disapproval.

'Yes, it's going to be so much easier with a proper timetable,' agreed Luke, munching away, and Megan made a mental note that she'd have to speak to him about his manners.

'You make sure you stick to it,' warned Darrow, his smile fading slightly. He became serious for a moment but Luke grinned, flashing his most mischievous of smiles. Megan felt her own heart-strings pull at the easy, affectionate bond that had grown between them.

'Hello,' she interrupted, eyeing Luke's plate, her eyebrows rising. 'Got enough to eat, Luke?' she mocked, with an air of disapproval.

She cast a covert glance in Darrow's direction. She now knew his secret—that he too had suffered the pain of rejection—and she wondered if he still felt as badly as she did. He had changed from the immaculate suit he had been wearing into a pair of snug-fitting jeans that seemed to fit like a second skin. A plain polo shirt added to his attractiveness. That was how she remembered him—casual and relaxed, not the high-powered businessman he had become.

'He's a growing lad, Megan,' teased Darrow, ruffling Luke's hair affectionately, and Luke grinned in response.

'You not eating?' asked Darrow. He saw Megan's hesitation so linked her arm. 'Come on, I'm sure I'll be able to tempt you,' he said as he escorted her over to the large brick barbecue. 'Grab us a table, Luke,' he called back over his shoulder. 'We like to eat like civilised people,' he joked.

'You two seem to be getting on well,' she commented coolly, surprised by the feeling of jealousy that she had to squash.

'Yes, I tore him off a strip for that fiasco when he was lost, but he apologised and it's in the past,' explained Darrow as he steered Megan through the people. She liked the feel of his possessive arm through hers.

'Luke apologised?' she repeated incredulously. 'That's a first.' Megan laughed, flashing Darrow a smile which he returned, making her stomach flip as the present seemed to fade away.

'He's mature for his age,' Darrow said, unaware of the twirl of panic that spiralled through Megan's body. She had carefully avoided being too definite about Luke's age. Darrow wasn't very good with figures, but he certainly wasn't so bad that he couldn't work out a term of pregnancy.

'Yes, I suppose he is,' agreed Megan, remaining noncommittal as she idly picked up a plate and moved to the selection of sizzling hot foods.

'You'd better take an extra chicken leg for Luke. He loves that chilli sauce—the hotter the better,' said Darrow as he helped himself to a large venison steak. Megan looked up, mildly surprised.

'You certainly have got to know him.'

'I thought I'd better.'

'Why?' asked Megan sharply, facing him in agitation.

'It seemed like a good idea,' he said, clearly ignoring

the tension that seized every muscle in her body. 'He's a great kid,' he added, sensing her disapproval of the situation and not quite understanding why.

'That still doesn't answer my question—why?' she persisted.

'Because you were right. I couldn't admit it at the time, not even to myself, but I was harder on Luke than the others because I resented him—resented the fact that he's your husband's son,' he confessed. 'I had to make amends, to see him as a unique individual instead of some reminder of you loving someone else,' he finished bitterly, and Megan stiffened at the injustice of the remark.

She wanted to believe him, to think his straightforward explanation was that simple, but she still didn't trust him. Besides, she had read that book. His love for Carrie was undeniable; it had screamed out from every line. It was he who had stopped loving, never she, and yet he seemed to blame her. Maybe his experience with Carrie had given him a jaundiced view of women? she thought.

'It's a beautiful day for a barbecue,' she said, forcing a smile on her face. She decided not to rise to the challenge he had thrown her. Otherwise she would have to admit that she had read the manuscript, and she wasn't prepared to do that until she had some good news about it.

'Yes. We're not always this lucky—quite often we're rained off and I quickly have to think of alternatives,' he said with a gentle smile as they wove back to their table.

'Such as?' asked Megan, intrigued, but not failing to notice a few envious glances from some of the women because she had Darrow's undivided attention.

'Well, today it's an American theme,' he told her as

he rested his hand on her back, steering her through a crowd of noisy children. She could feel the heat of his hand and tried not to react to it, but she couldn't help herself. Despite the revelations about Carrie, her feelings were unchanged. 'If it rains I'll just change the theme.'

'What do you mean?' she asked. It was a completely new idea to her, but she could tell by the tone in his voice that it was something that excited him.

'A Mexican party—the band would be in costume, playing suitable music, the room would be decorated in the national colours and the food would reflect the country. For instance guacamole, chilli, tortillas and enchiladas.'

'Sounds even better than the barbecue,' laughed Megan. She enjoyed Mexican food and the idea of a theme party really appealed.

'Maybe if you came back next year?' Darrow suggested lightly, but there was a wistful strain to his voice that Megan immediately detected.

'Perhaps,' she answered, shrugging. She doubted it, though. It seemed unlikely that there was any future for her here. She knew that no one could replace a first love, and his heart belonged to Carrie. He said nothing more about it and Megan was grateful; her emotions were all confused and time was running out. She and Luke were due to leave in four days, and she still hadn't told him— the time had never seemed right. Luke leaned over, helping himself to a handful of crisps as Megan sat down, and she frowned at him.

'You'll be sick,' she chastised, slapping his hand away as he attempted to help himself to some more.

'I'm a growing lad,' he complained with a rueful grin, then added for extra conviction, 'Darrow says so.' He looked back at Darrow for his approval and Darrow didn't fail him, but grinned back, making Megan feel quite redundant.

She concentrated on her meal. The sun was hot and Darrow and Luke were engrossed in some conversation about football—something she knew and cared little about. It seemed so natural, sitting here in the sunshine, just like any other family, she thought, glancing briefly round at the other holiday-makers.

'You OK, Megan?' Darrow broke into her reverie. She seemed unusually quiet, and he knew that that could often mean she was deep in thought. She looked up, squinting against the sunlight, her delicate skin already beginning to glow and a pink colour already covering her cheeks.

'Fine. I was just thinking how much I'm enjoying myself. I don't know whether I'll want to go back to London and to work,' she added, her face creasing in a grimace.

'You've enjoyed your holiday, then?'

'Is that a professional enquiry or a personal one?' Megan teased back, but she was curious to know his answer.

'Both,' he told her, with a ready smile that was dangerously sexy, and she wondered if he knew the effect he was having on her.

'Yes, I've enjoyed it,' she confessed, and, despite everything, she had. Luke was so much better, and for that alone she would always be grateful to Darrow. He had helped him through a difficult patch, when all she had seemed able to do was exacerbate the situation.

'Good. I'm glad, Meggie. I think you deserved the rest,' he acknowledged, and she knew he was sincere. Darrow never said anything unless he meant it. She smiled back, almost hating the way they could so easily slip back into the closeness they had known before.

'I'll go and get it, then,' cut in Luke as he clambered

over the bench. Megan's eyes followed him, disorientated.

'What's all that about?' she asked Darrow, as he obviously seemed to know and was nodding with approval.

'We thought we'd have a game of frisbee,' he told her,
ignoring the look of horror on her face. 'Luke told me
you enjoy it,' he teased lightly.

'I think ''enjoy'' is rather a strong word to use,' she
laughed. 'It was just that the tiny flat we lived in had an
even tinier garden and football was out of the question,
so I bought him a frisbee instead, and then was forced to
play to convince him that it was as good.'

'Did it work?' Darrow asked, and he was smiling, but
she saw the flicker of concern in his eyes and was
touched by it.

'No; I was forced to buy a house with a proper garden,'
she admitted, her laughter carrying on the warm midday
air, and she felt more free than she had done in years.

'Come on,' Luke called from a grassy hill, brandishing
a bright orange frisbee in the air. Megan groaned, but
Darrow was not prepared to let her stay sitting down. He
grabbed her arm and pulled at her, cajoling her to join
in, and despite her reluctance she stood up.

'I've just eaten,' she protested, but her pleas fell on
deaf ears.

'It will be better if you run it off,' Darrow invited as
they climbed up the hill to meet Luke. Megan paused,
turning to look at the view. It was wonderful—the lake
lay at the foot of the hills. She felt Darrow's arm drop
casually over her shoulder, his warm breath caressing the
side of her face when he spoke.

'It's beautiful, isn't it?'

'Yes, it is. My mother painted a wonderful landscape
of it. She must have sat somewhere near here,' she an-

swered, her voice tinged with sadness. And although the picture had always been very special to her she knew that now it would mean even more.

Darrow drew her close, allowing her body to lean against his muscular frame for support, and he knew that she was crying. Silent tears ran down her face. It was an indulgence that Megan rarely allowed herself, but somehow she couldn't stop. Darrow didn't speak; he just held her gently in his arms, his strength and power a source of comfort to her without the banality of words.

'Come on, lazybones,' Luke called, forcing Megan to dry her tears and put a smile back on her face.

'I don't know where he gets the energy from,' she complained, her feelings back under control now.

'At least he's better now,' commented Darrow, realising that she wanted a change of conversation and as always responding to her needs. Their hands slipped naturally into each other's, and Megan forced any thoughts of her mother firmly to the back of her mind, with all the other painful memories she wanted to forget

'The holiday has been marvellous for him; I've seen a real change,' she admitted, casting an appreciative smile at Darrow, and he squeezed her hand in return.

'Not for you, though?' he asked her, a frown of concern flickering across his brow.

'I did have other things to handle,' she reminded him gently, not telling him that the real problem was him being here and raking up all the past memories.

'Have you made any decision about your mother's house?' It was a polite enquiry, but Megan sensed the fine thread of tension that ran through his words and wondered where it originated from. She shrugged, raising her shoulders in an expressive gesture of indecision.

'I feel attached to it,' she said, forcing a lightness into

her voice that she did not feel. 'God only knows why!' she exclaimed, raising her eyes to heaven. Darrow knew that her home life had been unconventional.

'Well, it was your home for a long time,' he explained understandingly. The pressure on her fingers increased and the sharp tug of physical attraction she still felt for him stirred within her.

'I guess,' she said simply, pulling her hand away and pretending it was so that she could run. She felt the need for some physical release, and running was all she was prepared to do. Darrow kept up a steady pace at her side, turning to face her.

'When will you stop running away from me?' he asked.

'I'm not,' she replied hotly, but her cheeks flamed at his suggestion, it was so accurate.

'Aren't you?' he persisted, a glint of scepticism shining in his amused eyes.

'No,' Megan snapped, moving swiftly away, calling to Luke as she did so.

'Are you afraid, Meggie?' he taunted softly in her ear as she reached out to catch the frisbee, determined not to be affected by him.

'Afraid?' she repeated, allowing a puzzled look to form on her face before she turned away to toss the frisbee back to Luke. 'Of what?' Her green eyes focused on him, cool and aloof.

'Of me,' he challenged, knowing an explanation was unnecessary but enjoying the banter.

'Of course not,' she replied, a little too quickly, and she caught the amusement in his eyes. He knew her too well, and that angered her. He could gauge the way she was feeling with total accuracy, which was rather unnerving.

She was glad of the distraction of playing but after half an hour she fell exhausted on to the soft, warm grass, Darrow settling down by her side, his arms crossed under his head as he lay back to enjoy the sun.

'I'm getting old,' confessed Megan in a ragged voice, her breath coming in short pants.

'Me too,' agreed Darrow, but there were no signs of exertion—he seemed perfectly at ease.

'I'm going for a swim with Martin,' Luke informed them.

Megan lifted her arm, shielding her eyes from the brightness of the sun. 'You're joking!' she exclaimed, unable to believe her son.

'No,' he replied, equally surprised. 'I want to cool off,' he said, his voice fading as he walked away.

'Thank God he's gone,' admitted Darrow with a heartfelt sigh of relief. 'I didn't want to lose face but I couldn't stand the pace,' he laughed.

Megan gave him a sharp dig in the ribs. 'You were enjoying every minute.' She laughed as he gave a mock-cry of pain.

'I suppose I was,' he agreed with good humour, moving a little closer to her. Megan caught the scent of him, mingled with the fresh smell of the green grass and the warm sweetness of the nearby heather. It was so easy, with eyes shut against the sun, for the years to fade away and for her to be a young girl again.

'Aren't you supposed to be doing something?' she asked Darrow. Lying here sunbathing was far too dangerous. She knew her barriers would be down as she relaxed, and she knew now that he had never loved her—not really. His heart belonged to Carrie.

'Such as?' he asked lazily, his voice as warm as the sun.

Megan laughed. 'I don't know—you're the owner; surely there's something for you to do?' she admonished him, yet she wanted him to stay; it was so comfortable.

'Day off,' he murmured, leaning up on his elbow and watching her closely. Megan instinctively sensed his action and kept her eyes firmly shut, though her heartbeat increased its tempo.

'Yes, it's a day off and I plan to enjoy myself.' He clambered to his feet as he spoke, stretching his hand out to Megan. 'Come on,' he cajoled as he looked at her lazy figure, already settling down to rest.

Megan's eyes flickered open and she viewed him with interest. He gave her a winning smile and her own lips parted in response. She took his hand and he yanked her to her feet; she slipped and briefly she fell against him.

'Oops—sorry,' she said, stepping back instantly, too aware of the shock-waves that had jolted her body when they touched. He kept hold of her hand, forcing her to look at him, and she knew that the hunger that shone in his eyes was mirrored in her own. Her lids flickered down to cover her desire, but Darrow had already caught the look of longing in her eyes.

'Let's walk,' he said softly, his voice husky and coaxing, and Megan nodded in reply, unable to speak in case her voice gave away the depth of her feelings.

They walked back down to the barbecue area. Most of the buffet tables had been cleared away and replaced with a large wooden deck. Several bales of hay had been tossed with a designer's casualness around the edges and a noisy string band was warming up.

'Let's dance,' he said, pulling her to the wooden floor. But Megan dug in her heels, refusing to move.

'No way!' she exclaimed, the very idea horrifying her.

'Come on, spoilsport, it'll be a laugh,' he said encouragingly as his grip tightened, determined to have his way.

'I can't,' she protested. 'I don't know how to,' she admitted with a shake of her head, but Darrow was merciless.

'Of course you can. Besides, we're told what to do— given instructions—so you'll be fine,' he coaxed.

Megan swallowed. The last thing she wanted now was any further intimacy with Darrow. He had crushed all her defences and she was weakening all the time.

The dancing was fine, once Megan mastered it, and she enjoyed the easygoing sway and constant change of partners as it prevented her being in contact with Darrow for too long. She didn't know whether to be delighted or to despair as the music slowed to a seductive beat and Darrow stepped forward as her next partner. She could not give him the satisfaction of refusing to dance—he would guess her reasons and delight in them.

He held her close—too close—his body swaying against hers quite deliberately as they moved together in a gentle rhythm. She cast a quick, hopeful glance towards the band, longing for a change in tempo, but there seemed no hope. One of the players was so lost in the music that his eyes were closed, as if in a trance.

'I prefer this type of music, don't you?' Darrow murmured huskily in her ear, the warmth of his breath making her stomach flip, making a reply impossible. His hand pressed into her back, firm and familiar, as his thighs moved seductively against hers, making her legs turn to jelly.

Her own arms wrapped around him even tighter. She needed to feel the strength of him. Her whole body ached for the intimacy they had shared so long ago. She could feel his strong, steady heartbeat thudding against her trembling breasts and she closed her eyes as she leant against him, revelling in the musky scent of his aftershave. She knew she should pull away now, put some distance between them, but she couldn't. She raised her head to suggest that they sit down but his face was too close, his lips already brushing against hers. She tried to protest but the effect was hypnotic, and all Megan did was moan softly.

'We're too old for this,' said Darrow, disappointed. 'Besides, I'm no exhibitionist. Come on.'

It was as inevitable as day following night, and Megan knew that she wanted to—wanted to fulfil all the desires he was arousing in her, those that she had buried deep away after he had left her.

She was grateful that he suggested his room, as there was no fear that Luke would find them. Not that she was ashamed; it was just personal—too personal to share with anyone. His room was as she had expected it, sparse and rustic. The bed was a large old Victorian one, with a huge, ornately carved headboard full of swags and flowers and berries, and a thick, antique bedspread, full of muted colours that reflected the hills around them—deep purples, dull greys and heathers, all on a mossy green background.

'It suits you,' Megan said, her eyes quickly scanning the room, noting the fashionable tartan wallpaper that was offset by a plain but dramatic border.

'Mmm,' Darrow replied, taking her back into his arms. 'But I haven't come here to discuss the décor,' he said, his lips drifting over her face, and her whole body tingled in response. She knew they hadn't, but it had just seemed more dignified to say something to break the sexual electricity that was fusing between them. She had counted the reasons why she shouldn't come, reminding herself of what had happened last time, but she knew there was no turning back, that this was what she wanted.

Their kisses deepened and became electric in their intensity, his lips devouring hers. Megan's body moved traitorously against his and she could feel the effect she was having on him, stirring him as her hips moved against his legs. She felt as if she was on fire; she burned with desire. She had forgotten how quickly he could ignite her, making her forget everything but the need to be totally fulfilled.

She arched towards him with an abandonment that made him groan. He was enticing her to greater and greater levels of excitement, his hand stroking over the rounded contours of her breasts in slow, seductive movements, the slowness only serving to increase her passion.

'Are you sure you want to go through with this?' he asked, his voice uneven and heavy with passion, and his breath coming in short, harsh rasps.

Megan opened her mouth to speak but the words were somehow lost in the moment, and all she could do was nod mutely.

'Are you sure?' he asked again, his voice stabilising but still ragged. He wanted an answer. He wanted her to be as sure as he was about this.

'Yes,' she gasped, the word barely audible as it became trapped in her throat, which was choked with a heady desire. He smiled at her reply, a wonderfully heart-stopping smile that pushed away any last remnants of doubt as the past rushed up to meet them.

They drew closer to the bed, reluctant to move apart, and she stroked her fingers lovingly down his face, enjoying the feel of its rugged contours under her soft fingers. His hands had dropped to her waist and his fingers pulled awkwardly at the button at the top of her jeans.

Megan assisted him, as eager as he to shed the clothes
that were preventing their skin touching. He slid the jeans
down her legs, pausing to allow her to draw her feet out,
then with deliberate slowness he rose from his haunches,
keeping his hands on her legs and stroking them slowly
upwards.

She trembled as his strong hands moved over her
thighs back to her waist, which he encircled with his
arms, pulling her close. He placed a soft, teasing kiss on
her nose and she wrinkled it in disapproval, lifting her
mouth to his hungrily. He laughed at her actions, somewhere deep in his chest. It was rich and full of tenderness
and brought an even greater intimacy to the moment.
Clothes were now a cumbersome nuisance and each of
them threw them away with quick abandonment, till they
stood silently, gazing at each other's body.

'You're as beautiful as ever, Meggie,' he said huskily,
his honey-warm tone like a caress. Megan smiled a little
shyly in response, and opened her arms for him. He
moved quickly—too quickly, almost colliding with her
as they fell back on the bed. His apology was lost as she
found his lips and began to kiss him, deep and warm,
full of the growing passion she was feeling. He groaned
as she pulled him even closer, his eyes glowing with a
dangerous twinkle. She ran her fingers through his hair
and it fell between them, soft and shining.

His fingers stroked over her body, taking in every inch,
as if following an old but familiar and loved map. His
touch was light, skimming across her hot skin, arousing
her more and more. A wave of raw hunger swept over
her as his hand stroked her inner thigh, coaxing her to
respond to him. Each and every touch was filled with a
slow tenderness and he murmured her name as he lightly
kissed her face.

He moved over her till his body covered hers completely, her erect nipples pressing against the dark mat of hairs that covered his chest. She could feel the strength of him pressing against her and she moaned in anticipation. He rose above her, to allow her to move against him till she wanted him completely, and then she pulled on his shoulders with an abandonment she had never imagined as she cried out his name in frustrated anger. He smiled as he began his slow decent, and she marvelled at his control as he entered her.

Their passion knew no bounds now. They were caught in a heady sea of passion that was forcing their bodies even closer together, till they moved as one being, fused together in loving union.

Megan gasped as she gave a huge cry of spent emotion and sank back on to the bed, fully satiated and amazed by the depth of passion she had just experienced. She felt exhausted, but never more happy than she was at that moment. She curled against him, secure in his loving embrace, and he placed a single tender kiss on her head before she fell into a deep and dreamless sleep.

It was the sound of the shower that woke her, and for a moment she was totally disorientated, confused as to her whereabouts. A faint blush of colour pinkened her cheeks as she heard the *en-suite* bathroom door open. Darrow stood there, his body damp from showering, his hair wet and swept from his face. A towel was draped around his flat stomach and it drew Megan's eyes; it was like an invitation.

A smile curled one side of his mouth as he read her thoughts and he shook his head, as if amazed by her audacity, but he still joined her. Megan had been leading a celibate life too long; she was hungry to experience

every delight he had to offer, and she was willing to show
him the depth of her love for him.

This time their lovemaking was wonderfully slow, Megan taking the time to explore his body, to reacquaint
herself with him. She paused, her fingers faltering as she
felt a faded scar running down his side. She felt his body
tense as she lightly drew her fingers across it and she
wondered how it had happened. But she was not going
to spoil the moment by asking. He would tell her in his
own time, and till then she would keep a lid on her burning curiosity.

'Care to share a bath with me?' he asked wickedly as
she lifted herself from him, smiling with the satisfaction
that she had given him pleasure.

'Mmm, that sounds wonderful,' she agreed, slipping
from the bed and tiptoeing over to the bathroom.

Bathtime had never been such fun as they soaped each
other, then rinsed the water away, splashing like children
and laughing as if nothing mattered in the world but that
moment.

The shrill ringing of the telephone disturbed their play
and Darrow padded back into his bedroom.

A chill of dread wrapped around Megan's heart. She
could tell something was wrong—terribly wrong. The
tone of his voice was cold and serious, lacking the
warmth and laughter they had just experienced. He came
back to the bathroom, his face ashen, and he leant on the
doorjamb for support. The bath-water suddenly seemed
cold—icy. Megan stepped out, her heart thudding out a
desperate death-knell as she caught the grim look on his
face.

'Darrow? Darrow, what's happened?' she asked,
frightened by his stillness, the quietness that seemed to
have entered his soul.

'My mother...' he began, then he turned his back on her and Megan's heart shrank within her. She knew Janet had promised to keep her secret, but had she changed her mind? She stared after him, her heart sinking.

CHAPTER TEN

DARROW sank down on the bed, his shoulders slumped, as if he had the weight of the world on his shoulders. He looked up slowly as Megan came into the room. His eyes lifted to hers, full of sadness and regret, and Megan felt tears prick against the back of her eyes.

'Why, Megan? Why?' he asked softly, shaking his head in defeat.

Megan rushed to his side. She had to explain, to tell him how desperate she felt, how she couldn't have stood subjecting her child to the misery she had been through.

'I only saw her this morning—she seemed fine then,' he continued, his voice a sad mixture of confusion and disbelief. He jumped to his feet, casting a weak smile in Megan's direction as he scrambled into his clothes.

'I'm sorry, Megan, but you do understand—I have to go.'

Megan stared at him, totally at a loss. She had no idea what was going on but she felt a momentary relief that it obviously didn't concern Luke.

'Darrow!' she exclaimed. 'What on earth is going on?'

For a moment he looked puzzled, as if he thought she should know, then he gave her a sheepish grin.

'Oh, I'm sorry, Meggie. It's my mother—she's had a heart attack. That was Dad on the phone. He's at the hospital—I'm to meet him there,' he explained hurriedly as he ran a quick comb through his hair.

'Oh!' Megan gasped, genuinely shocked. She had always liked Janet; she had been so kind to her, so full of fun. 'I'll come with you,' she said, not waiting to dry herself and already grabbing for her clothes with agitated fingers. She could remember what it had been like with her own mother—that cold, empty feeling—and her eyes clouded with sorrow for her own grief.

'No, Megan,' Darrow said softly. 'It will only rake up painful memories for you. I have my father there, and besides, there's Luke to consider.'

Megan relaxed. He was right, of course, and she felt a stab of guilt, because in that moment she had forgotten all about Luke—she had only thought of Darrow.

'Come here.' Darrow smiled, taking her in his arms. The warm flare of passion was so easily ignited between them, and they kissed softly, drawing away reluctantly. 'I'll be back—promise,' he told her as he opened the door, blowing her a kiss, and Megan felt her heart contract. He had promised before, she remembered, and she faltered as she thought of history repeating itself, then quickly she suffocated her doubts and smiled at him.

'I know.' She nodded in agreement. 'I hope Janet will be all right,' she added truthfully as he closed the door behind him.

Megan dressed, her body still glowing in the aftermath of their lovemaking. She smiled to herself as she pulled on her clothes, each movement bringing back the memory of their desire for each other, and her stomach flipped with the thought.

She ran back down to her lodge, the wind whipping her hair from her face, her heart pumping fast as she increased her speed. She felt so happy, so alive—more alive than she had in years. She was exhilarated, bursting with life, and she knew why. The past was behind them and the future looked better than it had done in years.

*　　*　　*

Time hung heavily on Megan's hands. The phone remained silent—she constantly cast covert glances at it, willing it to ring, but it remained silent. She was grateful when Luke announced that he had been invited to the pictures with a neighbouring family, so would be going out soon; she wanted the time alone to assess the whirlwind events of the day. She wanted to hear Darrow's voice, to be reassured that she had not made the same mistake again.

Megan dived for the phone the moment it began to ring.

'Megan.' His voice was as gentle as silence, a sweet sound that washed over her like a balm.

'Hello, Darrow,' she said breathlessly as her heart thudded painfully against her chest, bursting with emotion. 'How's Janet?'

'Comfortable,' he said, quoting the doctors in an ironic tone. 'We won't really know anything till tomorrow. There are a series of tests to be done so I'm staying here,' he explained. She understood but was still disappointed.

'Yes, it's for the best. Besides, you couldn't leave your father,' she told him, trying to sound gracious and unconcerned that he was not coming back.

'Well, you can imagine what he's like,' Darrow said, and she could. They were the most devoted couple she had ever known.

'I hope he'll be OK—and how are you?'

'Coping, but missing you,' he said, and she could imagine the smile that was curling his lips as he spoke, the tenderness that would be shining in his eyes, and her heart soared within her.

'Missing you too,' she admitted softly, her eyes filling with unshed tears.

The call didn't last long—it was always difficult to

monopolise a telephone in a hospital corridor; every person had an urgent call to make.

Megan caught Luke watching her, a look of concern on his face. She knew why. They never had any secrets and he could see a change in her—her eyes were brighter, her lips curled in a soft, permanent smile and she hummed quietly, unable to contain her joy.

It was late afternoon two days later before the telephone rang again. Megan snatched it from its cradle, convinced that it was Darrow. She longed to hear his voice, to have him confirm how much he loved her, to reassure her that Janet was all right.

It wasn't Darrow, but the sudden wave of disappointment that initially swept over her was quickly replaced by excitement when she heard the familiar voice of her friend Sue. It was a thrill to hear from her, and to have her agree with Megan's view. It *was* a good story, she said, and she would be interested at least in talking to the writer.

Megan was delighted. Now more than ever she longed for Darrow's return, to tell him the good news. Everything was working out so well—like a dream come true.

She had to wait a further two hours before she heard the rap on the door. She knew it couldn't be Luke—he had gone fishing—so she raced to the door, flinging it back with such force that it slammed against the wall with the impact.

'Darrow,' she gasped, falling into his open arms and hugging him tightly. 'How's everything?' she asked, but she could tell it was good news. He looked brighter than he had when he'd first received the call.

'She's recovering. It's not as bad as we first thought.

It seems it was more a severe angina attack, really,' he explained as they both made their way inside.

'Thank God,' murmured Megan, and she meant it. 'Would you like a drink?' she asked as he followed her out on to the sun-kissed balcony. He looked at the bottle of champagne chilling in an ice-bucket and his eyebrows rose in surprise.

'Shall I do the honours?' he murmured in a smoky tone, and her slow smile matched his as she handed him the towel-wrapped bottle.

'Be my guest.' Her voice was breathless from the slow-building tension that their closeness created. She watched his fingers peel away the silver foil, easing the cork away with an expert's skill. The sudden pop made her jump, and she quickly held the long, fluted crystal glasses out to catch every drop. The white foam bubbled upwards, threatening to overspill, but Megan's mouth quickly covered the rim of the glass and she swallowed deeply, enjoying the cool dance of bubbles over her tongue.

'Are we celebrating something?' asked Darrow, taking a sip and nodding his head in approval of her choice.

'Yes,' she replied, a smile of triumph curling her lips as she saw the look of surprise in his eyes. But he nodded in understanding.

'My mother kept rambling on that you had something to tell me, but I didn't really take much notice,' he admitted, settling himself down on one of the chairs, crossing his long legs over each other casually and staring out at the beautiful scene before him.

Megan couldn't sit; she was too excited. She knew she wanted to tell him about the book first. She hadn't quite worked out how to tell him about Luke, but she knew how much easier it would be now.

'It's about your book,' she began, her excitement almost uncontainable, but Darrow remained unmoved, a frown of puzzlement forming on his brow. He cast her a quick look.

'What book?' he asked, a sharpness in his voice she had not expected, but she disregarded it as she hurried on, wanting to tell him the news.

'Your book. Sue, my friend who works in publishing, telephoned this afternoon. She couldn't put it down— she's read it and likes it,' Megan enthused, unaware of the grim expression that was forming on Darrow's face. She continued breathlessly, 'She wants to talk with you— thrash out a few ideas. Isn't that great?' she finished, taking a large mouthful of champagne. Not that she needed it; she was already drunk on excitement and joy.

Darrow put his glass down firmly on the table and he stood slowly, facing Megan. His expression was troubled, as if he was fighting some inner battle, and Megan guessed it was fear, lack of confidence in his ability. The thought of having a publisher interested in his book must be pretty daunting, she thought.

'I don't know what you're talking about, Megan,' he told her grimly, his voice too quiet, too controlled. The granite-hard impassivity of his face alerted her to his anger, but she couldn't understand its origin.

'The other morning, when I was in your office, I had to look for a file,' she explained patiently, realising that she had not made herself clear. 'I found a manuscript—'

'It's nothing,' he snapped, cutting in and stopping her flow of explanation. 'Just a few ideas. I meant to throw it out,' he concluded, as if the conversation was at an end.

'Well, I'm glad you didn't—' she began again, till he

fixed his eyes on her, steel shining from their dark depths. She hated this quiet anger, an anger that was building all the time, adding to the tension that was developing between them, robbing them of the tenderness she had expected.

'You didn't read it?' he asked, already knowing the answer, and his whole body had tensed rigid as he tried to control his emotions.

'From start to finish,' Megan said with a smile. He needed reassurance, that was all. She remembered how sensitive he'd been about his writing. 'It's very good,' she told him, but he stared at her in horror and disbelief. 'Honest, it really is good Darrow,' she rushed on. I really liked it.'

He stared at her, his soft blue eyes slowly clouding till they were as black as the night, full of bitterness. He pushed his hair from his face, needing to do something to release the tension that gripped every muscle in his body.

'Good? Good?' He repeated the adjective in disgust, his voice full of venom as he stepped away from her. Megan felt the cold chill as he put some distance between them and her heart shivered. She couldn't understand. She had wanted to help him, and now it was all going sadly wrong.

'I thought it was…' she argued, but there was a tremble in her voice now, almost tinged with doubt, as she looked at him, searching his face for some tenderness but finding none. His face was set in a grim, uncompromising mask.

'You had no right to read it,' he bit out, glaring at her with unconcealed distrust. It hurt Megan to admit it, but it must be Carrie. He still loved her so deeply that he saw this as an intrusion. And she had foolishly thought they had a future together.

'I'm sorry. I didn't realise it meant that much to you.' She was hurt now and hitting back, annoyed with herself as much as him for being such a fool, for falling for the same trick twice. Her temper was fuelled by his attitude. She felt he had betrayed her yet again. 'I never would have sent it away if I'd known,' she spat at him.

'Sent it away?' he echoed, as if now everything was finally falling into place.

Megan took a deep breath. She knew it was hopeless now; she could see he wasn't impressed by her actions, but she had to tell him the whole story. 'I sent it to a friend, Sue, in London. She's been in publishing for years and I thought she'd be interested in publishing it.'

'Publishing it!' spluttered Darrow, as if the very idea was anathema to him. 'It's not for publication. It's not for everyone. It's mine and private,' he said possessively, his indignation infuriating Megan. There had been a time when all he was interested in was having a book published, but not now, and she knew why. It was all for Carrie, and how that hurt.

'I can see it means a lot to you, but there was a time when getting published did too,' she countered, trying to suffocate her own pain that was fuelling her anger and despair.

He looked at her almost sadly, shaking his head as if disappointed by her actions. 'You don't understand. I don't want it published,' he said firmly, seizing her arm in a torturous grip so different from the gentle caresses she had experienced from him before.

She shook herself free, her eyes bright with anger, the green pools flaring with harsh lights of pain. 'You can't mean that, Darrow,' she taunted cynically. She tossed her head arrogantly, forcing him to deny the most important thing in the world to him. She was stunned when he did.

'I can and I do, so you'd better get it back—and quick. And in future I'd thank you not to poke your nose into my business,' he declared in an ominously low tone.

'I was helping you,' Megan protested hotly.

'Well, I'd thank you not to help again,' he said, towering over her in momentary rage before he turned his back on her, stiff and angry.

'I don't understand.' She laughed almost bitterly. 'It's a great story...' She would have continued but he swung back round, his face twisted in rage.

'Damn you, Meggie,' he cursed her. 'It isn't a story. It happened to me,' he roared at her, but she could hear the pain in his voice and it left her stunned, staring at him, her eyes wide pools of innocence. 'Well, not quite like in the book,' he admitted quietly.

'I know you loved Carrie...' she said, forcing the jealousy from her voice and trying to replace it with understanding. But she just evoked his temper even more.

'Loved Carrie?' he echoed, looking at her in utter horror. 'You still don't understand, do you?' he snarled as he seized her shoulders in a tight hold that pinched into her skin. 'I kept my promise, Megan. It was you who went off and married someone else—had his child,' he said bitterly. 'Or is Luke his? Don't tell me all that passion the other night was his exclusively? Was your marriage promise to him as worthless as the one you made to me?'

Megan's palm hit the side of his face with such force that his head recoiled with the impact. Her hand stung, her arm vibrating with the shock of her action.

'Get out!' she screamed, hating him with all the passion she had loved him with the other night. 'Get out!'

she screamed again, looking at his reddening cheek with sudden alarm as she thought of the possible consequences of her action. Not that he could have hurt her any more than he had just done.

He looked at her, his eyes narrowed into steel lights, and for a moment they both just stayed there, staring at each other with total hatred. Then he spun away from her, pulling open the door with such strength that it shook the house. He paused and turned.

'I want my book back,' he said, his voice low and threatening, before he turned away.

Megan expelled the air that had been trapped in her lungs in a low whistle as she heard the door slam. She felt sick, her legs weak, and she sank back into her chair. The two half-empty champagne glasses seemed to mock her, the drink now as flat and as meaningless as all her dreams. She didn't realise how long she sat there, staring over the lake with lost empty eyes, too numb to think.

'What's for dinner?' Luke's voice broke into her thoughts, and Megan shivered as she realised that the sun had disappeared long ago and now a cold breeze was blowing.

'I haven't really thought,' she answered automatically. 'What would you like?' she asked distractedly as she picked up the two glasses and moved back into the kitchen to rinse them under the tap.

'Not bothered,' came the muffled reply as Luke searched inside the fridge for something to eat.

'Luke,' said Megan, suddenly turning to face him, 'we only have a couple more days, and instead of staying here perhaps it would be nicer to go and stop at Granny's house. What do you think?' she asked nervously, longing to get away, to put as much distance as she could between her and Darrow.

'When?'

'Now,' replied Megan impulsively. 'Let's just dump everything in the cases and go,' she added with more enthusiasm now. The idea really appealed. Luke picked up on her mood and his mouth widened into a boyish grin.

'Yes, let's. It'll be fun. We can get a take-away from the village and a bottle of cider,' he said, adding details that made it even more exciting to him.

'You bet!' agreed Megan. This was how it always had been, just her and Luke, and it was enough for her, she told herself without conviction.

Three hours later they were sitting in front of a burning fire, the remnants of their meal scattered across the floor. Megan emptied the last drops of cider into her glass and sighed wearily. This was the only time she had ever used this place as a haven and yet it seemed oddly appropriate. Maybe her mother had been unconventional, refusing to marry her father, but at least she had never suffered the pain of rejection Megan had to bear.

She blinked away the tears that threatened to fall. She was not going to indulge in self-pity. In two days she'd be back in London, as far away as she could be. She knew she might have to move. If Janet told Darrow the truth he was bound to come looking for them, and she was equally determined that she would not be found.

'How about going to York tomorrow? We can have a look round, take in the cathedral, and if we take an overnight bag we could stay,' Megan suggested. She wanted to stay away from Rannaleigh as much as she could.

'Sounds great,' agreed Luke. 'I feel as if I've been cut off from civilisation.' He laughed, clutching his chest. 'I long for the smell of pollution, concrete under my feet, the frantic noise of a busy street.'

Megan joined in his laughter at Luke continued, warming to his theme. 'Rush-hour traffic, crowds of harassed people pushing me.'

'All right, its a deal. Let's turn in now so we can make an early start,' encouraged Megan. She wanted to be away, to rid herself of all the unhappy memories that surrounded this place.

The two days they spent in York were marvellous. The city was steeped in history. It was late when they returned to Megan's mother's house. Luke was tired out; the constant sightseeing and the long drive had taken their toll, and he fell into bed, exhausted.

Megan began to pack, carefully folding the clothes and placing them away neatly. She worked steadily, hardly noticing the time till she heard a tap on the door. She stiffened, casting a quick look at the clock. It was very late. Outside it was dark and she suddenly felt fearful; the cottage was so isolated. Tentatively she crept towards the door. She jumped when the knock came again, louder this time, and a familiar voice called out.

'Megan? Is that you?'

Megan sighed with relief, opening the door to face Darrow. He looked awful. His eyes looked red-rimmed and sunken, as if he hadn't slept, and there was the dark hue of a five o'clock shadow on his face. His dark hair was tousled, and Megan immediately thought of Janet.

'Darrow, what's happened? What's the matter?' she asked anxiously, stepping away from the door to allow him to enter.

'Megan,' he gasped. 'Thank God you're here. I thought you'd left. I've been looking for you.' His eyes looked desperate, haunted, deeply troubled, but Megan couldn't understand why.

'What is it, Darrow? Why were you looking for me?' she asked, troubled herself.

'I'm sorry, Meggie, I blew my top. I should have taken the time to explain. It was the shock, that's all. It brought it all back and I wanted to bury it, leave it all behind in America, not bring it home here to sour everything.' He rushed it all out, but Megan understood; she knew the pain of losing someone.

'It doesn't matter,' she said bravely as she twisted the knife in her wound. 'It has nothing to do with me. I was wrong to interfere,' she admitted, hating this conversation and wondering how much more pain he was going to inflict upon her.

'But it does concern you,' he said with growing impatience as he took her in his arms and pushed her gently on to a chair. Megan stiffened. She didn't want to know, to have him explain his depth of emotion for someone else. He saw her doubts flickering in the cool depths of her frightened eyes. 'I love you, Meggie,' he said softly. 'I've always loved you.'

Megan stared at him, nonplussed. The only word she uttered was, 'Carrie?'

'I met Carrie the first week I arrived in America. She was one of the many teenagers at the campus—a real cute kid. Unfortunately she was totally infatuated with me, only I couldn't see it—I was still pining for you. I should have seen it. She'd do anything for me, just like Luke would, and like him she took unnecessary risks...' His voice faltered for a moment and Megan reached out and clasped his arm.

'What happened?' she asked quietly, knowing that this was a different story from the one she had read.

'There was a climbing accident.' His voice shook with emotion but he continued. 'She fell,' he said simply, shutting his eyes as the vivid image of Carrie's body floating through the air flashed through his mind. 'I tried to save her, but I was hurt too.'

Megan recalled the scars she had felt on his body, the tiny one on his face, and knew they were the result of this accident. But it wasn't the physical scars that still hurt him and she whispered his name in sorrow. She could now understand why safety was so important to him, and why Luke's behaviour had made him so angry.

'I'm so sorry, Darrow,' whispered Megan, still finding it all rather hard to take in. 'But surely you weren't to blame?'

'No, I was exonerated, but she was badly injured—I was too. That's why I didn't write for so long, by which time I'd heard the news about you and Karl,' he finished sadly. 'So as soon as I could I began to write for television. It wasn't what I wanted but I needed the money. I felt I owed Carrie that much, to help with the hospital fees, and I no longer had you.'

'How's Carrie now?'

'She never fully recovered. She spent the last couple of years of her life in a wheelchair. She wanted me to marry her but I couldn't. She was always a child in my eyes. I felt I had treated her badly enough without living a lie, so I stayed with her till she died. That was when I decided to come back. So the book wasn't about Carrie, it was about how I felt when I lost you—and I thought I had done again. Where were you?'

'We went to York and stayed over,' she explained, throwing her arms around him and drawing him towards her, her lips hungrily covering his face in a series of comforting kisses.

'Where's Luke now?' he said, a suggestive smile curling his sensuous mouth.

'In bed.' Her heart was thudding painfully against her ribs as she realised what he meant.

'Good.' He grinned, pulling her closer, but Megan pulled away. At last the right moment had arrived, and she was not about to lose it again.

'No, Darrow. About Luke…'

'Luke will understand,' he told her, drawing her back into his arms, and her defences crumbled. 'I think he realises how I feel about you. I want to marry you, Meggie, and I want Luke to become my son legally,' he said, hoping he hadn't overstepped the mark.

'He is.'

'What?'

'Luke is already your son, Darrow. There was no marriage to Karl—there was never anything,' she began, hurriedly trying to explain as a look of disbelief flooded Darrow's face.

'Mine?' he said numbly.

'I knew I was pregnant the day you told me about your scholarship. I couldn't stop you going—I knew how much it meant to you. I thought you'd be back, but your letters spoke of Carrie, then stopped all together…' Her voice trailed away as she now understood what had happened.

'No doubt your mother added to it. She never liked me, or any man, that much,' he said grimly, but Megan jumped to her defence.

'She was my strongest ally in the end. I had no one else. I just didn't want Luke growing up with the same stigma I had, so I made the Karl story up,' she confessed, suddenly feeling a little foolish.

'My poor Meggie. In many ways we were both so young—so foolish,' he said wistfully.

'And so much in love,' she added, and at least now she knew that was true, and her heart flipped within her at the thought.

'Yes, we did both keep our promises after all,' he said, his mouth searching for hers and kissing her lightly on the lips. 'Are you going to marry me, then?' he asked, his smile deepening the creases in his face, and Megan paused for a while to tease him.

'Only to give my son a name,' she joked, and laughed uproariously as Darrow lunged at her, tickling her till she screamed for mercy.

'I can't wait to tell Luke,' Darrow said, unaware that the noise Megan had made had woken him up and he was already standing bleary-eyed at the door, eyeing them both with amused interest.

'Tell me what?' he asked curiously.

'We're going to be married!' Darrow informed him, wrapping an affectionate arm around Megan's shoulders.

'That's neat,' Luke replied, which was the nearest he ever got to a compliment. 'Goodnight, Mum,' he called as he left them both together, then added, 'Goodnight, Dad.'

Darrow groaned and fell on to Megan's breast. 'Is that huge double bed still in the spare room?' he asked with a wicked grin.

'Yes,' replied Megan with a knowing smile.

Darrow yawned noisily and stretched. 'I could do with an early night.'

'So could I,' agreed Megan, but she still had some energy left and, she felt sure, so did Darrow.

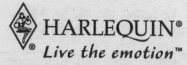

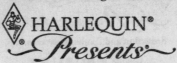

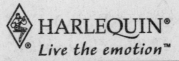

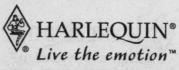

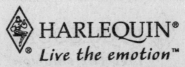

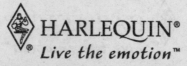